Temple Israel Library
Minneapolis, Minn.

Please sign your full name on the above card.

Return books promptly to the Library or Temple Office.

Fines will be charged for overdue books or for damage or loss of same.

What Happened to
Heather Hopkowitz?

Other Novels by Charlotte Herman

What Happened to Heather Hopkowitz?

by Charlotte Herman

E. P. DUTTON   NEW YORK

Library of Congress Cataloging in Publication Data

Herman, Charlotte.   What happened to Heather Hopkowitz?

Summary: When the parents of fourteen-year-old Heather
go on a month cruise, she goes to stay with Orthodox
family friends and decides to change her life.
[1. Jews—United States—Fiction]   I. Title.
PZ7.H4313Wh   1981   [Fic]   81-5111
ISBN 0-525-42455-5   AACR2

Published in the United States by Elsevier-Dutton
Publishing Co., Inc., 2 Park Avenue, New York, N.Y. 10016

Published simultaneously in Canada by Clarke,
Irwin & Company Limited, Toronto and Vancouver

Editor: Ann Durell   Designer: Susan Lu

Printed in the U.S.A.   First Edition
10 9 8 7 6 5 4 3 2 1

for my cousin
Morris Katz
a way of saying thanks

1

I am not the same Heather Hopkowitz I used to be. One day my mother and father sailed off to the Caribbean, and I turned into someone else.

They had decided on the cruise because my father, Harvey Hopkowitz, who is probably the top oral surgeon in all of New Jersey, said he was sick and tired of looking in people's mouths and needed a change of scenery. It was a toss-up between Mexico and the Caribbean.

"They're both IN this year, but I think I'd prefer the Caribbean," my mother said. She was examining the travel folders showing sunshine, food, laughing faces, and bikinis.

My father sneaked a look at the bikinis.

"Hmmm. I think I'm inclined to agree with you, Abbey. The Caribbean looks great to me."

I was thrilled. "The Caribbean! Fantastic. I can hardly wait!"

"Sorry to disappoint you, honey," my mother said. "But this trip is just for your father and me. First of all, we'll probably be going in December, and you'll still be having school for most of the month. And secondly, it would be too expensive to take the two of you."

By "the two of you" she meant me and my brother, Shawn. Shawn is five years old and walks on his tiptoes. He was sneaking looks at the bikinis too.

It didn't matter what my mother was saying about school and expensive. I knew that the sole reason for not including us in their plans was because it's not considered IN to drag your kids along on exotic vacations.

"Where will you be dumping us while you're away?" I asked.

"We won't be dumping you anyplace," my mother said. "Shawn will stay with Aunt Gloria, and you . . . well, we haven't decided about you yet."

"Why can't she stay with Aunt Gloria too?" Shawn asked.

"Aunt Gloria lives too far from school," my mother explained.

"I'll stay with Audrey or Roseann," I said.

"I was toying with that idea too."

"I'm not so sure," my father said. "Why don't we think about it?"

Audrey and Roseann are Audrey Oppenheim and Roseann Gross, and they're my closest friends. I told them about the cruise later that evening when we went bowling. It was a Friday night, and we always went bowling on Friday nights. It was sort of an eleventh commandment for us: Thou Shalt Go Bowling on Friday Nights.

"Maybe I'll get to stay with one of you," I said on the way to the bowling alley.

"Hey, wow. That's great!" Roseann said. "If you stay with me, we'll have a ball. We'll have the place to ourselves practically."

Roseann's mother works every day, and her father is a steak salesman who's out of town most of the time. There's hardly anyone home there.

"We'd have a ball at my house too," Audrey said. "You'd blend in with the rest of us and never be noticed."

Audrey is one of seven children, and there's always somebody coming or going in her house.

"We haven't really decided anything definite yet," I said, thinking that I'd prefer to stay with Roseann and have the house to ourselves and gorge on steak.

We changed into our bowling shoes while Roseann took a survey of the boys who were hanging out at the alley.

"A real bunch of nothings," she concluded.

"They're the same bunch of nothings who come here every week," Audrey said, trying to stuff her foot into a size-too-small shoe.

"I don't understand it, Audrey," I said. "How can

3

you remember the boys who come here every week when you can't even remember your shoe size?"

"You can't forget faces like those," she said, as if we were such bargains.

Audrey is slightly built, has stringy hair, and wears glasses. Roseann is short and chubby, and I—I am just ordinary. There is nothing unusual or spectacular about me. Except maybe my eyes. I do have these spectacular deep blue eyes that I inherited from my grandmother—my father's mother.

My bowling was not too spectacular that night. I made what would have been an enviable golf score, though. We changed back into our street shoes and went out for cheeseburgers and malts. While we were walking, we periodically checked to see if we were being followed. As usual we weren't.

"Maybe we ought to switch bowling alleys," Audrey said after we settled ourselves in a booth at a fast-food restaurant a few blocks away.

"There's no other alley close by," I said. But I was thinking, as I bit into my cheeseburger, that Audrey was on the right track. We needed a change. I'd been feeling that way too lately.

"I've got it!" I said. "We'll give up bowling for a while and try roller skating."

Roseann went into hysterics. "What? Give up bowling? Are you kidding?"

"Don't get so worked up, Roseann. I just thought we might find a better variety of boys at the roller rink."

"We can do both," Audrey suggested.

4

"Sure," I said. "Bowl on Fridays, skate on Saturdays. Double our chances. It'll be a new experience for us."

"Too expensive," Roseann said. "My father doesn't sell that much steak. Let's stick to the bowling."

When I got home, I found Shawn parading around the living room in his little jockey shorts. He was walking on his tiptoes—the way he always does when he's in his underwear. Maybe that's how he developed such shapely calves. How I admired those calves. No, that's not entirely true. I was jealous of them. Insanely jealous. What does a five-year-old boy need with shapely calves when his fourteen-year-old sister has sticks for legs?

"Where is everyone?" I asked. I was anxious to settle this matter about where I would be spending an entire month out of my life.

"They're in the den. Daddy's looking at the pictures of the ship and Mommy's typing 'Deserted.' "

"Deserted" is one of the many true-confession stories my mother's been writing recently. The full title is "Deserted by My Husband Because I Can't Cook." Some of her other titles include "I Found My Husband at a Garage Sale" and "Hostage," which is about this harried housewife who can never get out of the house because she can't afford a sitter, and can't take her kids anyplace because they're a bunch of brats.

My mother decided on a writing career after one of her Letters to the Editor was published in the local paper and she saw her words in print. None of her confessions have been published yet, but she's determined. She spends most of her days writing, composing catchy titles for prospective stories, and waiting for the mailman.

She was pulling a sheet of paper out of the typewriter when I walked into the den.

"My best story yet," she said triumphantly.

"Does her husband ever come back to her?"

"She doesn't *want* him back."

"Good for her," I said. "I've decided to stay with Roseann."

"Well, I don't see why not." She fished a paper clip out of her wastebasket and clipped the pages of "Deserted" together. "If it's all right with the Grosses, of course. What do you think, Harvey?"

My father looked up from the deck of the S.S. *Rotterdam.* "There's not enough supervision at the Grosses'."

"So who needs supervision?" I asked. "Roseann gets along fine without any."

"Mrs. Gross is usually home by six," my mother said.

"Usually is not good enough," my father answered.

"Okay, so I'll stay with Audrey," I said. So much for steak and independence.

"They've got enough kids in that house without adding another one."

"They wouldn't even notice me," I told him.

"I want you to be noticed."

"Then what do you suggest?" my mother asked my father.

"I'll stay home and take care of myself," I said.

"I was thinking of the Greenwalds."

My mother placed "Deserted" on her desk. "The Greenwalds?"

"You mean Shani?" I asked. Shani Greenwald lives around the corner, and when we were small we used to spend a lot of time playing together. But we go to different schools, so except for summers and vacations, we don't see each other that much.

"I've known Nate Greenwald since we were kids," my father continued. "Our families go way back together."

"I know all that," my mother said, "but . . ."

"Hey, I've got an idea," I interrupted. I looked straight at my father. "Why don't you stay with Nate Greenwald and I'll go on the cruise with Mom."

"That might be the solution," my mother said, and laughed.

"You two are hopeless," my father said. He placed the travel folders on the end table and sat back on the couch.

"What I'm saying is the Greenwalds are a good family. And I know they'd enjoy having Heather stay with them."

"She couldn't possibly feel comfortable there for a whole month," my mother said. "I'm surprised at you for even considering the idea."

"Why wouldn't she feel comfortable? She likes Shani."

"Oh, Harvey, come on now. Do I have to spell it out for you? The Greenwalds . . . well . . . they're different. They're so . . . so . . . Jewish."

7

I knew what my mother meant. We're Jewish too. Only not in the way the Greenwalds are. No two Jewish families could be so different. The Greenwalds observe the Sabbath and keep kosher, and Shani goes to the Hebrew high school instead of the public high school. We never went in for any of those things.

My mother didn't have much of a Jewish upbringing. Actually she had none. So, unlike Shani, I've been brought up to observe Halloween and Valentine's Day and to ignore the Jewish holidays, except maybe for Yom Kippur, a day of prayer and fasting. We liked to go to Temple in the morning and out to lunch in the afternoon.

My father, on the other hand, comes from a more traditional background. But when he left home, he didn't bother to take any of the traditions with him.

The only *Jewish* Jewish person in our family in recent times was Grandpa Morris Hopkowitz, who was living in a convalescent home, recovering from a stroke. My father visited him every Sunday so he wouldn't be too lonely. Most of the time Shawn and I went with him. We were his only family. Grandma Hannah Hopkowitz died when I was about five. Sometimes my mother would accompany us, but she was usually either too busy writing or found other excuses for not going.

She and Grandpa had a rather strained relationship which began either when she tried to persuade my father to change his name from Hopkowitz to Hopkins when they were married, or when she refused to let me call Grandpa *Zayde* as he had asked. She preferred Gramps. And that's when my father put his foot down. Under no condition would his daughter go around calling her grandfather Gramps. So they compromised and settled on Grandpa.

"Heather's got nothing in common with Shani," my mother continued.

"Why don't I just go to the Caribbean with both of you and we'll solve the problem?" I asked.

"Okay," my father said.

"Okay? You mean I can go with you?"

"No. I mean, okay, why don't we ask you how you feel about staying with the Greenwalds."

"Oh."

"You like Shani, don't you?"

"Well, sure, but . . ."

"Then it's settled."

"Harvey, that's not fair. You know she'd have a much better time with Audrey or Roseann. These girls have gone through school together, Girl Scouts, Brownies, everything."

"Just because she stays with Shani doesn't mean she won't have plenty of opportunities to be with Audrey and Roseann," my father said. "And in the meantime I'll know she'll be in good hands. How about it, Heather?"

"I don't know," I said. "I never even thought of Shani. I'll have to get used to the idea."

I certainly knew Shani well enough. And I liked her. I guess in a way I was even fascinated by her. There was something of a mystique that surrounded her. Especially when we were small. There were certain foods she couldn't eat, and certain days were more important to her than they were to me. And she had Hebrew books in her house that she could actually read. And Shani could write in Hebrew too. She could read and write a strange and ancient language while I was just trying to cope with my ABC's. Still, a whole month of all that Jewishness.

"I don't know," I said.

"Trust me," my father said.

"Well, maybe it would be okay. I probably wouldn't mind staying with her. I could look upon it as a learning experience. The only thing is the food problem. No bacon. No Twinkies."

"No Twinkies?" my mother asked.

"They're made with lard. I remember that Shani never ate Twinkies."

"See what I mean," my mother said. "Imagine not being able to eat Twinkies."

"Yeah," I said. "Imagine."

"I survived an entire childhood without Twinkies," my father said.

"Well, you didn't know any better," I told him, and my mother and I both laughed.

"Like mother like daughter," my father said, and shook his head.

And so it was decided. A month-long cruise to the Caribbean beginning the first week in December. For three months before the trip, my mother and I had a ball every Saturday buying out all the clothes

10

in Bergen County and dining at different restaurants.

"We're buying enough stuff to last you the entire month without having to wear the same thing twice," I teased one Saturday during lunch.

"I know," she said. "And isn't it fun? When I get back we'll do it again. Only we'll mostly window-shop, because I won't have any money left."

On the last Saturday of our shopping spree, my mother treated me to a new nightgown, a few tops, three pairs of jeans, and some underwear.

"Always try to look your best when you're there," my mother said.

We were all up early the Friday my mother and father left. The suitcases were packed and lined up in the hallway. Tote bags spilled out into the living room.

"It looks like you're going away for a year," I said when I went into the kitchen. My mother was fixing bacon and eggs—the last request of a condemned prisoner—for breakfast, and my father and Shawn were already sitting down at the table.

"Better fill up on the bacon and try to make the taste last for a month," my mother said, and she set the platter of bacon and eggs in front of me. I took two large helpings of bacon, skipped the eggs, and poured myself some milk.

"Maybe I can come back here and make myself some when I get hungry," I said.

My father started laughing. "You've got to be kidding. When was the last time you did any cooking?"

"Probably around the same time she cleaned up her room," my mother said.

"Well, you never can tell. I might become desperate."

"I'd rather you didn't experiment with the stove while we're away. I'll make it up to you when we get back."

"You two are acting like this is the end of the world," my father said.

All this time Shawn hadn't said a word. He just sat there, resting his head on his arm and poking holes in his scrambled eggs.

"What's with you?" I asked.

He didn't answer. He just kept sitting there, looking pathetic.

"He doesn't want us to leave," my mother said. "Isn't that right, dear?"

His blue eyes under their long lashes were filled with tears. And when he blinked, they squeezed out of his eyes.

"I'll miss you," he said.

My mother reached across the table and touched his hand. "We'll miss you too, honey. But the time will pass quickly and we'll write to you from every port."

"And I'll try to call you every day," I promised.

Shawn looked at me and sniffed. "Heather, can't you come with me to Aunt Gloria?"

"I can't, Shawn. I've got school, remember? But Aunt Gloria said she'd fix it so we can see each other on Saturdays or Sundays. And Christmas vacation for sure. It won't be so bad."

"We'd better get moving," my father said. And he and my mother got up to clear the table.

"Have you packed yet?" my mother asked me.

"I just threw a few things together. I can always come back whenever I need something."

"Be sure to double-lock the door each time you leave," my father reminded me. "And don't touch the lights. I've got the timers connected to them and they're set to go on and off automatically."

"And you'll be sure to check the mail, dear, won't you?" my mother asked. "Not that I'm expecting anything. 'Deserted' came back yesterday."

"It did? How come you didn't say anything?"

"I was too crushed. Anyway, I've decided to put that rejection out of my mind for now. I'm determined not to let anything spoil this trip. Oh, Harvey, I hope you didn't forget my seasick pills."

"Don't worry about a thing. I've got three different brands for you. One of them is bound to work."

"Get your things together, Shawn," my mother said. "Aunt Gloria will be by for you in a few minutes."

Shawn ran to me and we hugged and kissed. And then we all hugged and kissed and said our good-byes.

"Have a good time."

"Take care of yourself."

"Write."

I put on my jacket, gathered up my books, and started toward the door. And just as I walked out I heard my father call, "Give my best to Nate."

And then my mother, "Heather, if things get too sticky, call Aunt Gloria and start your vacation early."

"I will, Mom. Thanks." It was comforting to have a plan of escape. Just in case.

2

Roseann was waiting for me on the corner. Even without seeing her face I could recognize her by her furry brown coat. Whenever she wears the coat she resembles a koala bear, and she looks so cuddly I sometimes get the urge to pick her up and give her a squeeze.

She greeted me with her clenched fist raised in a power salute along with her favorite expression, which I think she borrowed from her mother. "Thank God It's Friday." She began blowing on her hands to warm them up. "Where is that Audrey already? She's late."

"Of course she's late," I said. "If she wasn't late she wouldn't be Audrey." And that was true. Audrey

is always late. Audrey is always running, always losing, always forgetting.

"Hey, Heather, you sure you won't come with us
tonight?" Roseann asked.

"Oh, Roseann, I wish I could. But how can I? I
have to be at Shani's house."

"But Heather, it's Friday. We always bowl on Friday."

"I know we do. But how can I just walk out on the
Greenwalds like that? Especially my first night over
there. And you know Shani won't go bowling on Friday night."

"You should have stayed with me."

"I wanted to. You know that."

As I was talking, I caught a glimpse of a slight figure flying up the street.

"Oh, there she is. Finally."

Audrey came running toward us, hair blowing with
the wind, glasses askew, bandage on nose, and pant-
ing. She was pressing a hand against her chest.

"Oh, I hurt. All that running. I was halfway here
. . . forgot my math book . . . had to go back. Oh,
I hurt."

"What happened to your nose?" I asked.

"Oh, that. You wouldn't believe it. I walked into a
door yesterday. The stupid electric eye didn't work.
It was a horrendous experience."

Horrendous. It's Audrey's latest word. To Audrey,
everything is horrendous. Her toothaches are horrendous, her sinuses are horrendous, and the food in
the school cafeteria is horrendous.

16

"Heather's not going with us tonight," Roseann said.

Audrey perked up. "For God's sake, why not?"

"Because tonight's the night I begin staying with Shani," I said.

"Remind me."

"Audrey, you're impossible. I must have told you a hundred times already. My mother and father are going to the Caribbean and I'm spending the month at Shani's house, starting today after school."

"Oh, yeah. Now I remember. Can't you make up some excuse to leave?"

"Yeah, get out of it," Roseann said.

"Look," I told them, "I would if I could. But I can't. Maybe next Friday, but not tonight."

After school I stopped at the house to get rid of my books and to pick up my tote bag, which contained all the things I'd need for the night. It was blue denim and had a Levi pocket sewn on one side. Then I went over to Shani's house.

I knew Shani Greenwald even before I met her. I met her in a sandbox. Before that, our grandmothers pushed us side by side in baby carriages, and then in strollers. We grew up like that, in the beginning. Through our grandmothers. Our grandmothers are both gone now, but we've remained friends.

I rang the bell above the nameplate that read BARBARA AND NATHAN GREENWALD, and made a face into the peephole. It was the same face I'd been making ever since I was tall enough to reach the peephole. I crossed my eyes and let my tongue loll

17

out the side of my mouth. I waited for Shani to answer.

Where was she already? My eyes were getting out of focus and my tongue was getting dehydrated.

Finally the door opened.

"Hello, Heather. Come on in."

Uh oh. I refocused my eyes. "Hello, Mrs. Greenwald. I thought you were Shani."

Shani's voice came from the top of the stairs. "Heather, is that you? Come on up."

She met me halfway up the stairs and took my bag.

"Shani, how could you do that to me?" I asked her as we ran up to her room. "You were supposed to answer the door. I just made the most disgusting face at your mother."

"Think nothing of it, Heather. I do that to her all the time. She's used to it by now. Oh, I'm so glad you're here. We'll have lots of time to catch up. Come on in and put your things away."

The nice thing about Shani's room is that even though it's a lot more orderly than mine, it's not overly neat, and I feel comfortable whenever I'm there. I thought the room was gigantic when I first came here to play with Shani, but through the years it seems to have shrunk in size. She used to share the room with her sister, Beth, but Beth went off to study in Israel, and now she has the place all to herself.

Her room is decorated in blue and green, and lining an entire wall is her collection of books and knickknacks. Shani has done considerable traveling and has souvenirs from such historical sites as Williamsburg, Gettysburg, Washington, D.C., and Independence Hall.

I remember the time Shani was a serious rock collector. But evidently she's given up rocks and is into smelling nice. Where rocks once cluttered her dresser there were around fifteen bottles of colognes, perfumes, and eaux de colognes.

"I've made room for you in the closet," Shani said. "And you can have the top drawer of my dresser."

Shani stood and watched while I confidently removed my underwear and nighties from my tote bag and placed them in the drawer. Confidently because I had all that new stuff my mother bought me. And it was a good thing, too. My former undergarments were stained and yellowed with age, and some of the elastic was loose and hanging. She watched me put everything away.

"Gee, Heather, I forgot to remind you to bring a skirt for tonight," Shani said.

"A skirt?"

"Yes. For *Shabbos.*"

"Oh, Shani. I didn't even think of bringing one. It never crossed my mind." I could just picture myself attending a Sabbath dinner in a pair of blue jeans. I looked around for the telephone so I could call Aunt Gloria and start my vacation right away.

"It doesn't matter," Shani said. "You can wear one of mine." She took my hand and led me to the closet. With great flair, she flung open the door. "As you can see, plenty of skirts. Take your pick."

19

The girls in Shani's school are not allowed to wear jeans or slacks. So Shani has quite a nice selection of skirts. I chose a navy corduroy to go with the navy and white sweater I was wearing.

My sweater was a bulky knit, and very flattering. You could not tell how flat-chested I was underneath. I try to wear lots of bulky knits. Sometimes even in the summer. When everyone else is wearing halters and tube tops, there I am, suffering heat prostration in my bulky knits.

Sometimes it worries me that I haven't developed yet. But then I look at Shani and I don't feel so bad. She doesn't have anything either. In fact, almost none of my close friends do. I make it a point not to be close to anybody who has much more than I. With the exception of Roseann, who was close before she grew to such outstanding proportions. She burst forth suddenly, without warning, and she can't be blamed for that.

The one thing Shani *does* have that I don't is a perfectly clear complexion. I've often wondered if it was due to her kosher diet. And I hoped, as we stood together in front of the mirror fixing ourselves up, that the month's stay at her house would clear up my complexion too. That would at least compensate for all the good stuff I would be missing.

"Shall I wear my English Shani or my Hebrew Shani?" Shani asked, holding a necklace in each hand.

"The English, definitely."

"Why definitely?"

20

"I can't read Hebrew."

She lifted the hair from her neck so I could fasten the clasp of her silver necklace with the Shani dangling from the chain. Shani has always loved personalized jewelry and has all kinds of pins, pendants, and rings with her name or initials in Hebrew or English. Her habit of collecting things like jewelry and now cologne makes her an easy person to buy presents for.

"Look at us," Shani said, "you in blue and me in green. We match my room."

"It takes you to notice something like that," I told her, and we sprayed each other with cologne and made faces in the mirror. Faces in the mirror. Something we hadn't done in a long time. Maybe we never really grew up.

The smell of dinner was drifting up the stairs and my stomach started to gurgle.

"Did you say something?" Shani asked, and laughed.

"Well, I didn't. But the small voice inside me said I was hungry."

"Let's go down and see if we can speed things up," she said, and led me down to the kitchen.

All around the kitchen there were aluminum pans filled with food, and Mrs. Greenwald seemed to be trying to decide which ones to put into the oven. There were square-shaped packages of aluminum foil and round-shaped packages on top of the counters and the table.

"Your whole kitchen looks like it's wrapped in

foil," I whispered to Shani. We were standing at the doorway looking in. The kitchen seemed to have shrunk in size too.

"Well, you know my mother. She doesn't get the chance to cook often, but when she does, she cooks and freezes enough for months. Her big problem is that she never puts on labels, and she can't remember what she's got in the packages."

Mrs. Greenwald teaches English at Shani's school. And every day when she comes home, she pulls complete meals out of the freezer. My mother does her cooking the last minute. But she can whip up some pretty good meals in no time. And if she can't come up with anything interesting, we meet my father at the door and take him to a restaurant.

Mrs. Greenwald slipped a pan into the oven. Then she turned around and smiled at us. She's slim and pretty, and her hair is brown and straight like Shani's. Except that her hair is short, and Shani's is long. My hair waves in all the wrong places and always seems to be at an in-between stage. Mrs. Greenwald doesn't have anything on top either.

It is a weakness of mine to make offers to people and hope they won't take me up on them. It's easy to be generous that way.

"Can I help you with something, Mrs. Greenwald?"

"Oh, no thank you, Heather. Why don't you sit down and relax. Dinner will be ready in a few minutes."

"Why yes, Heather. Thank you. You can help Shani set the table."

Rats!

It's not easy to set the table at the Greenwalds'. I had tried it once before and had become terribly confused. They have all these different sets of dishes and silverware. They have six sets of dishes that I know of. Kosher people use separate dishes for meat meals and separate dishes for dairy meals. The Greenwalds have meat and dairy dishes for every day, meat and dairy dishes for company or the Sabbath, and meat and dairy dishes for Passover. They also have six sets of silverware to go with the six sets of dishes. They have separate pots and pans too, but I didn't consider that a problem since I didn't do the cooking.

The table in the dining room was covered with a gold-colored cloth, and on it were the two loaves of challah, a silver wine goblet, and two pairs of silver candlesticks. Shani led me to the buffet, where I helped her take out the dishes. They were white and had delicate blue flowers along the border.

"These are pretty," I told Shani.

"Thanks," she said. "We use them every Friday night. Could you get the silverware?"

"If I can find it," I said, and went into the kitchen. Another thing that always fascinated me was their silverware. The meat and dairy silverware were kept in two different trays. One blue and one red. But I could never remember which was kept where. It was like a guessing game.

"It's in the blue tray, right?"

"No," Shani said. "That's the everyday dairy."

"The red tray, then."

"No," Shani called back. "That's the everyday meat." We were playing the game.

"Why don't you just tell her where it is and make it easy for her?" Shani's mother said.

"Yes, I wish you would," I said. "I don't think I'll ever get the hang of this."

Shani opened the top drawer of the buffet and took out the silverware. "Sure you will, Heather. In a few days you'll know where everything is."

Mrs. Greenwald came into the dining room.

"The table looks lovely, girls. You did a nice job. We'll light the candles in a few minutes."

I went into the living room to look around at the books and admire the paintings on the walls. There were some oils and watercolors by obscure artists— at least they were obscure to me—but they were soft and subdued and pleasant to look at. So unlike the paint-by-numbers, velvet paintings, and other gaudy wall hangings you'll find at Roseann's house. Over Roseann's sofa in the living room is an enormous painting of an ocean with gigantic waves crashing against the rocks. I get seasick whenever I look at it.

"I hope they meet with your approval," someone said.

I recognized the voice and turned around. It was Nate. My reason for being here. Not only is he my father's old buddy, but he's also the principal of the school Shawn will be going to in a few months. He has dark hair, and dark eyes so deeply set that he always looks deep in thought. I remembered that I was supposed to give him my father's regards. I decided not to. The time didn't seem right.

"I've always liked them," I said. "And they don't get me seasick."

"Seasick?" he asked.

"Some paintings get me seasick if I look at them too long. These don't."

"I'm glad to hear that," he said.

Shani called to me from the dining room. "Heather, you want to light some candles? We've got extra holders."

"No thanks," I said as I went into the dining room. "I'll just watch."

Mrs. Greenwald covered her head with a scarf, and then she and Shani each lit a pair of white candles. With their hands they made circular motions above the flames. Then they brought their hands to their faces and covered their eyes for the blessing. Where had I seen that done before? Where?

Grandma Hannah. And all at once I was standing at a table in another house, at another time, long ago. And Grandma was making those same circular motions above the flames, and covering her eyes with her hands. From behind her hands came soft, low murmurs. And I was watching her and wondering what mysterious words she was uttering. Now she was looking at me and smiling. *"Good* Shabbos, *Heather,"* Grandma Hannah was saying.

"Good *Shabbos,* Heather," Shani said, and brought me back. *"Shabbat Shalom."*

"Good *Shabbos* and *Shabbat Shalom* to you too," I said.

Mr. Greenwald poured us each some wine and recited the blessing, the *kiddush.* Then he recited the blessing over the challah. They certainly said a lot of blessings at the Greenwalds'. I thought of my mother. She probably would've gone into shock. I would have too, but the blessings helped muffle the gurgling sounds that were erupting from my stomach, and I was ever grateful. An especially loud gurgle came up as Mr. Greenwald cut the challah, and I offered an overenthusiastic *Amen.*

Mrs. Greenwald served chicken soup with these small white things floating around which I called won ton and which Shani called *kreplach.* We also had roast brisket with all kinds of side dishes I never tasted or even heard of before.

While we were eating, Mr. Greenwald got up from his chair. "Drinks anyone?" he asked.

"Thank you, Nathan," said Mrs. Greenwald. "I'll have tea."

"Make mine Coke," Shani said.

"How about you, Heather?" Mr. Greenwald asked.

"Milk, thank you," I said.

A silence filled the room. I felt my face grow hot. I looked down at my plate and stared at some little brown things sautéed in onions and mushrooms.

Milk! How stupid of me. Didn't I know that Shani never drinks milk with meat? That the Bible forbids it? Even when we were small and played restaurant, I always ordered milkshakes with my hamburgers, while Shani ordered Cokes.

"No thank you," she once said to me, the waitress, when I asked what flavor milkshake she wanted with her hamburger. "I don't drink milk with meat."

How could I have forgotten? I looked around for the phone again. I would call Aunt Gloria and arrange for my getaway. Except that the Greenwalds don't use the telephone on the Sabbath. So how could I, right in front of them? My mother was right. I never should have come here. Give my regards to Nate. Ha!

Shani patted me on the shoulder. "That Heather is some great kidder."

"I sure am," I said. "Especially when I'm drunk."

"How about some Coke instead?" Nate asked. He smiled and poured some into my glass. I think he knew I was not a great kidder.

The next few minutes were filled with small conversation.

"So . . . your brother is staying with an aunt, I hear."

"Yes he is, Mr. Greenwald."

"Your parents were probably very excited about the trip."

"Yes they were, Mrs. Greenwald."

"The Caribbean must be lovely."

"Yes it must."

Then, just as I was finishing up the last of the little brown things, Mr. Greenwald suddenly burst into song. Like in a TV commercial, or some grand musical production where right out of the blue, people start walking down the street singing and waving to each other as if it were the most natural thing to do, he started to sing. And so did Mrs. Greenwald and so did Shani.

They sang a medley of Hebrew songs, none of which I had ever heard before. But after a while I was able to join in on a few *la-la-la*'s.

When we were all sung out, Mrs. Greenwald looked around at the three of us.

"It feels good to have four at the table again. It's nice having you here, Heather. It's been lonely since Beth left."

"She'll be back by the end of summer," Shani reminded her.

"I know," Mrs. Greenwald said, and sighed. "But before I turn around you'll be wanting to go too."

"Are you really planning to go to Israel?" I asked Shani when we were upstairs.

"Well, I'd like to someday," she said, slipping out of her clothes and into her Wautoma, Wisconsin, nightshirt. "Hey, Heather. Maybe you could come with me. There are all kinds of work-study-travel programs. Maybe we can even live on a kibbutz for a while. We'll learn the language and get a feel for the land."

I could see it all now. *"Mom, Dad, I have an an-*

nouncement. I've finally decided where to go after high school graduation."

"Oh? Where is that, dear? Harvard? Vassar? NYU?"

"No, I'm going off to Israel to live on a kibbutz. An Orthodox kibbutz. I'll learn the language and get a feel for the land." I had to stifle a laugh.

"It's an idea," I said, and then I got into my nightshirt too. A gift from Audrey and Roseann, it was pink and had an enormous pair of red lips on the front, with Hot-Lips Heather written around it. Some hot lips! I have never been kissed by a boy, and if it should ever happen to me, I'd probably faint dead away.

"Did you enjoy the dinner?" Shani asked.

"Oh, yeah. I really did. It was an experience, too. All those blessings."

"You think that's a lot?" Shani said, and flopped down on her bed. "We've got prayers and blessings for everything. There are prayers you say before you go to sleep, when you wake up, when you go on a trip. There's even a prayer for after going to the bathroom."

"What? You've got to be kidding," I said. And I laughed so hard my hot lips quivered.

"It's true," Shani said. "I know it sounds funny, but you've really got to be grateful for something like that. You'd be surprised at all the people who can't go normally."

"Yeah, I suppose," I said, and climbed up to the

top bunk. The telephone rang. It rarely rings in Shani's house on the Sabbath, and when it does, it goes unanswered. It kept on ringing. Maybe Aunt Gloria was trying to reach me.

"Doesn't it bother you with the telephone ringing like that?"

"No."

"I could never let a phone ring in my house without answering it," I said. "It would drive me crazy."

We talked for a while longer, and then, because the Greenwalds don't turn the lights on or off on the Sabbath, the automatic timer turned the lights off for them. I thought about my own house, with the timer going off and nobody there to notice.

A warm, delicious aroma wafted up the stairs and hovered around my bed.

"It smells as if the dinner is still cooking," I said to Shani.

"That's the *cholent*," she said. "It's a kind of stew. It'll cook all through the night and we'll have it tomorrow after *shul*. That is, if you'd like to come with us."

"Sure, I'll come," I said.

Shul. A synagogue. An Orthodox synagogue yet. Now that, I thought, just before I dropped off to sleep, should really be an experience.

3

"Just look at all this discrimination," I said to Shani. "Haven't you people heard of equality for women?"

We were sitting in the women's section of the synagogue, and I was leaning against the shoulder-high divider that separated the men from the women.

"Oh, you mean the separate seating," Shani said. "It's not discrimination. It's just separating the sexes. So the men and women concentrate on prayer instead of on each other."

And with that sentence, we simultaneously turned our heads around so we could look across the divider and watch the boys sitting in the rear of the synagogue.

I noticed an especially nice-looking one leafing

31

through the pages of his prayer book. He was wearing a small blue skullcap on his sandy blond hair.

"Heshy Rabinowitz," Shani said.

"What?"

"Heshy Rabinowitz. That's who you're staring at."

"How do you know who I'm staring at?"

"Because every girl in school stares at Heshy Rabinowitz."

"You go to school with him? No kidding? I think I'll transfer."

"You don't have to do anything that drastic. I'll introduce you."

I couldn't get over how different this synagogue was from the one I sometimes attended on the High Holidays. In the first place, my parents don't call our synagogue a synagogue. They call it a Temple. *"Come, Heather, we're going to Temple."* And in our Temple, the men and women sit together, the men don't wear skullcaps or prayer shawls, and the services are in English. Not in Hebrew like it was in this one. And where was the organ? And the microphone? How strange. *"Hey, Mom, look where I am! Wait until I tell you all about this. My first Orthodox service."*

No, not my first. I had been to one before. The men's prayer shawls remind me. And the women's hats.

And I am back again, somewhere, running up the stairs. Up to a balcony where the ladies are sitting. Where Grandma Hannah is sitting, wearing a hat. And she puts her arm around me and gives me a book to read. Only I don't know how to read. So I just hold it and pretend, and listen to Grandma sing. Then I run downstairs to Grandpa Morris. And I sit next to him, running my fingers across his prayer shawl, feeling its silkiness. And I try to make braids out of the fringes, and he lets me. Then I see the Torah being carried down the aisle while everyone is singing. And the men are reaching out, touching the Torah with the fringes of their shawls, bringing the fringes to their lips. And I'm touching the Torah too, with my fingertips.

And then I have to leave.

"It's time to go back to Temple," my father says. *"Our visit is over."*

But I don't want to go to Temple. There's nothing doing there. I want to stay here, where there's a balcony.

"I wish there was a balcony here," I said to Shani.

"A balcony?"

"Like there was in the synagogue my grandparents went to."

"And mine."

"The same one, I think."

"Yes, it was the same," she said.

I don't have to pretend with Shani. We both know I can't read Hebrew. The only way I could keep track of the service was to follow Shani and do whatever she did. So when she turned the page I turned the page. And I read the English translation of what she read in Hebrew. When I got tired of doing that, I started to read the inscriptions on the plaques that were all around me. One of the stained-glass windows was DONATED BY THE SISTERHOOD IN MEMORY OF OUR BELOVED SYLVIA ZIMMERMAN. The chair in front of me was IN HONOR OF OUR PRESIDENT, MAX GREENSPAN. Even the *siddur*, the prayer book I was using, was DONATED IN HONOR OF BRUCE BIRNBAUM'S BAR MITZVAH. I had just finished reading my ninth plaque when the rabbi walked up to the pulpit. Half the kids got up and left.

During the break, Shani introduced me to a few kids and took me on a tour of the synagogue. When the rabbi finished his sermon, we went back to the service. I spent the remaining hour humming hymns, sneaking glimpses of Heshy, and listening to the announcements. I was glad to hear that Florence Rosenblum—whoever she was—was recovering nicely from her gallbladder operation, and that the Teitlebaums, who were celebrating their fiftieth wedding anniversary, were sponsoring the *kiddush* in honor of the occasion.

We concluded the service with the singing of "*Adon Olam*" and went into the Sheldon Perlmutter Social Hall for the Teitlebaums' *kiddush*.

The *kiddush* consisted of five different kinds of cake, gefilte fish, Carmel concord grape wine, and pickled herring with onions.

"Take plenty," Shani said, and piled too much of everything onto my plate.

I was just getting ready to dig in when a voice asked, "Do you want your onions?"

I looked up into the face of Heshy Rabinowitz and

I knew I would gladly share my onions with him. He had a slightly crooked front tooth and a slight bump on the nose which I thought lent character to his face.

"Oh, here. Take them all," I said.

While Heshy was transferring the onions from my plate to his, Shoshana Katz, a short dark-haired girl Shani had introduced me to earlier, came over and offered her plate of onions to Heshy. I had just begun to think I'd lost Heshy to another girl's onions when Shani came up to us and said, "Heshy, I'd like you to meet an old friend of mine, Heather Hopkowitz. Heather's staying with me for a whole month, so you'll probably be seeing a lot of her."

"Nice to meet you," Heshy said. "Maybe you'll join some of our youth activities. We've got a lot of things planned. Ice-skating, tobogganing, even a scavenger hunt at Newark Airport."

"When is all this exciting stuff supposed to happen?" Shani asked.

"As soon as we get another president," Heshy said. "As you know, our last two resigned."

"I'm thinking of running," said Shoshana Katz.

"I've got a feeling you'll be elected," Heshy said.

Shoshana edged over toward Heshy and gave him another onion slice. "Really, Heshy? Why do you think so?"

"Well, as far as I know, you're the only one running."

"Very funny," Shoshana said, and snatched the onion away from him.

35

I noticed a small white-haired man wearing a pin-stripe suit walking toward us. He was obviously the official candy man of the synagogue because all these little kids were tagging along beside him, tugging at his jacket. The response was a piece of candy wrapped in cellophane, a pat on the head, and a warning, "Don't run around with the candy in your mouth. You'll choke."

The candy man. Grandpa Morris was my candy man—and Shawn's. He was a magician. He could produce candy or gum in midair. Behold, an empty hand, a couple of magic words—*guggle muggle*—and voilà! Gum balls from behind the ears.

His pockets were bottomless. You could reach into any one of them and always come up with something. It was as if he had in each pocket a miniature candy factory that constantly replenished the supply, just when you thought you had exhausted it.

My mother and father were not as delighted with these candy factories.

"Please, Pa. You're giving them entirely too many sweets."

"Pa, come on. You know it's no good for their teeth."

"Ah, my son the dentist. What's a grandpa for?"

Shani waved to the little man and called to him, "Mr. Teitlebaum, you forgot about us."

"Yeah," said Heshy, as Mr. Teitlebaum approached, "you haven't given me any candy since my Bar Mitzvah."

"True," said Mr. Teitlebaum, shaking Heshy's

36

hand. "But if you remember, I was the one who showered you with all those little bags of candy on that day."

Heshy smiled. "For a sweet life. I remember all right, Mr. Teitlebaum."

We all wished him *mazel tov* on his anniversary, and when Shoshana Katz wished him another fifty years with Mrs. Teitlebaum, he clapped his forehead, gave out an *"Oy, gevald!"* and left us each a piece of candy along with his warning, "Don't run around with the candy in your mouth. You'll choke."

I finished off everything on my plate, said goodbye to Shoshana and Heshy, and left the synagogue with Shani, not knowing how in heaven I'd ever find room for Mrs. Greenwald's *cholent.*

4

I had long made up my mind to be the perfect guest in the Greenwald household. I would not overeat, make long-distance telephone calls, or give Mrs. Greenwald my dirty laundry. And if I had a severe stomachache, I would go home to use the bathroom. So it was that when the pickled herring started playing volleyball with the *cholent,* I went home to suffer in private.

I took a quick shower, threw wet towels around the bathroom to my heart's delight, and changed into another bulky knit.

Though the house was quiet, it was far from being empty. Original paintings by Shawn and Heather covered the walls and refrigerator, and scattered throughout the house were the clay vases, bowls, and

Popsicle-stick jewelry boxes from all those countless Mother's Days, Father's Days, birthdays, and anniversaries. Everything proudly displayed, not hidden away to be looked at and admired twenty years from now. My eyes rested upon a portrait of me that Shawn once made for my birthday. My arms are sticking out of my head. I remembered I had promised to try and call him every day. I ran to the phone.

"I knew it would be you," Shawn said, right after he answered the phone. "I was waiting."

"How are you, honey? I miss you."

"Me too. But I'll see you tomorrow. Aunt Gloria's taking me to a movie later—a Walt Disney one—and then we're going out for frozen yogurt. Hey, Heather, what do you call a skinny horse?"

"I give up. What?"

"A bony pony. Aunt Gloria wants to talk to you. Bye."

"Hi, are you lonesome?" Aunt Gloria's voice boomed out at me from the other end. She almost blew the wax right out of my ears.

"Oh, I'm okay. I stopped by the house to check on things, so I decided to call. When will I see you and Shawn?"

"We were just talking about that when you phoned. We're planning on coming by tomorrow and going out to visit your grandfather. It would be a heartbreak for him not to have visitors all month."

"Thanks, Aunt Gloria. Dad said you might be able to take us sometimes."

Aunt Gloria is my mother's sister. And I thought it

was especially nice of her to offer to take us to see Grandpa when she isn't even related to him.

When we finished talking, I went back to Shani's house.

I knew enough to knock on the door. I had never spent too much time with Shani on Saturdays, but I did know that you don't ring the bell on the Sabbath. My father taught me that long ago, on those Saturdays when he walked with me to Shani's house, he to visit Nate and I to visit Shani.

"We don't ring the bell on Saturdays," he had said. "So we'll just knock."

No one answered, so I knocked a few more times. Mr. Greenwald finally opened the door. The place was jumping. It was almost as if they were having a party. It's often like this on Saturday, Shani once told me. Especially when it's warm and it's good walking weather. People just drop by, unannounced, and visit over tea and cake.

"Come in, Heather," Mr. Greenwald said. "Shani and the others are upstairs."

Who were the others? I wondered as I walked up the flight of stairs to Shani's room. Heshy Rabinowitz? Shoshana Katz? I didn't have to wonder long. There was no mistaking Audrey Oppenheim's laughter. She sounds very much like a hen who's trying hard to get her egg out.

"So uugly!" Audrey was cackling. "Ugly, I tell you."

"Who's ugly?" I asked, walking into Shani's room. Roseann was sitting on Shani's bed, tittering.

"Oh, hi, Heather," Roseann said, in between titters. "We came here looking for you. We were just describing the two guys who tried to pick us up in the bowling alley last night."

"Yeah," Audrey said. "It's too bad you couldn't come with us. You really missed something. They were horrendous." She started to cackle again.

"Were you planning on going with them?" Shani asked me.

"She wanted to, except she had to be here," Roseann said. Roseann Gross has about as much tact as a laxative.

"Oh, Heather, I'm sorry about that. I wish you would have told me. You could have gone with them."

Shani is very sensitive. And very apologetic. She's always apologizing for something that isn't her fault. Like rain that spoils a picnic, or a crowded subway.

"I know I could have," I told her. "But I didn't want to." I looked pointedly at Roseann. "It's no big deal to miss a little bowling once in a while."

Roseann ignored my last remark and began leafing through her latest movie magazine, *Secrets of the Stars*.

"Hey, look at this," Roseann said, showing us an ad on the back cover of her magazine that pictured a well-endowed girl who got that way just six weeks after using an amazing new bust developer that's shipped to you in a plain brown wrapper for only $10.95, including postage.

"Say, let's see that one," Audrey said, grabbing the

41

magazine from Roseann. "'Transform yourself from a plain thirty-two-inch bustline to a gorgeous forty. Even though you have been flat-chested all your life, we guarantee a gain of one to three inches a week or your money back.' Say, how about that!"

"And you can have it sent to my house like you did the last time," Roseann said. "No one's ever home when the mail comes."

"Forget it," I said. "We're not being taken in by any more of those phonies. Our last experience should have have taught us a lesson."

"That's right," Audrey said. "For three dollars and fifty cents apiece we got an overgrown rubber band that broke in two days. It was a complete bust." And she laughed her head off at the pun.

"Maybe you should try barbells," Roseann said.

"That's for your biceps," Audrey told her. "Who wants to walk around with overdeveloped biceps?"

I was sure Audrey didn't know what she was talking about, but I didn't want to get into an argument about body-building.

"Oh, Heather, here. I have something for you." Audrey reached into her purse and pulled out an envelope that looked like it had traveled halfway around the world.

"What's this?" I asked. "A chain letter?"

"Open it up and see."

"A birthday card. That's really nice of you, Audrey. The only thing is, my birthday was two months ago."

"Yeah, I know. But I stuck it away in my locker

and forgot about it until I cleaned it out yesterday. It was a horrendous mess."

We spent the rest of the afternoon looking through an old *Guide to American Colleges* that belonged to Beth.

"I like to search through the book for unlikely places to go," Shani said. And that afternoon we chose the Colorado School of Mines for Roseann, and for Shani we selected the Catholic University of Puerto Rico. Audrey and I were undecided.

I went home after lunch the next day to check the house and wait for Aunt Gloria and Shawn to pick me up. I sat by the window and waited until the blue Volvo pulled up in front of the house. When I opened the door, Shawn flew at me as if we'd been separated for a year instead of a couple of days. I picked him up and swung him around, while he squealed and giggled.

"I helped Aunt Gloria bake a cake for Grandpa," Shawn announced when I set him down.

"And it's going to be the most delicious cake your grandfather ever ate," Aunt Gloria added when she popped into the house. And I do mean pop. Aunt Gloria pops and bubbles. She's so full of life and energy that she's already gone through three husbands. My father calls her the five-foot powerhouse. He didn't appreciate it any when I once suggested to him that maybe she's high on drugs—pep pills, or uppers, or whatever they're called.

"More likely it's her diet," my father once told me.

Aunt Gloria is big on health foods. She's part owner of the Back to Nature health food store in Teaneck.

"She's always been that way," my mother had answered him. "Even as a kid, she was a bundle of energy."

"What kind of cake did you bake?" I asked Aunt Gloria.

"It started out as a zucchini cake, but now we're not exactly sure," she said, and winked at me. She winked at me with her left eye—the blue one. Her right eye is brown. She's the only person I know who has two different color eyes. Aunt Gloria says that's because it's a very rare phenomenon. Audrey says you can achieve the same effect with tinted contact lenses.

When I was little I loved to hear Aunt Gloria's explanation of how her eyes got that way. "I used to have two blue eyes," she'd say, "but one of them turned brown because I ate too much chocolate." And then she'd say, "If you watch very carefully, I'll make my eyes trade places. But you've got to be quick, or you'll miss the whole thing."

Now Aunt Gloria entertains Shawn with these same lines. And no matter how many times he hears them, he laughs like crazy.

Shawn ran through the house to make sure everything was still there. Then he emerged from his room with some of his toys and said, "All ready. Let's go."

Convalescent homes. How they depress me. The smell of medicine, the way people sit around waiting for visitors. Or worse yet, the people who wait for visitors who never come. It's pathetic to hear people trying to explain to each other—or themselves—why their sons and daughters aren't coming that day. And that's why it was so important for me to be with Grandpa. So he wouldn't have to be one of those who had to explain.

We walked into the reception lounge where the benches were filled with the waiting ones. Aunt Gloria, who had never been there before, acted as if she were the head nurse. She went from person to person, saying hello, asking about their health and really caring, now and then taking a hand and reassuring someone that everything would be all right.

Grandpa was in his room reading. As soon as he saw us he broke into a grin and spread out his arms. Shawn flew at him with his foil-wrapped cake.

"Look what we brought you, Grandpa."

Grandpa kissed the top of Shawn's head and said, "Hmmm, what do we have here?"

"It's a surprise. It's a cake."

Aunt Gloria walked over to Grandpa and said, "It's made with zucchini, whole wheat flour, honey, and best wishes for a complete recovery."

"Thank you," said Grandpa, clasping Aunt Gloria's hand. "I like all those ingredients. Especially the last one."

Shawn reached into Grandpa's pocket and pulled out a piece of bubble gum. The candy man. Even in here.

"And how is my *shane maydele*?" Grandpa asked me, and I went to him and kissed his cheek. *Shane*

45

maydele. Pretty little girl. It's what he and Grandma always called me. They were probably the only people who thought I was a *shane maydele.*

"I'm fine, Grandpa. How are you feeling?"

"Now that you're all here, I feel very, very good."

"You look good too, Grandpa."

You look at Grandpa's face, his smooth skin and clear blue eyes, and you'd never believe he was in his mid-seventies. He looks more like sixty. You'd never believe that just three months earlier he had his stroke. It's only when he walks around and you see his slowness that you realize the full extent of his illness.

Shawn climbed up on Grandpa's lap. "Can you blow smoke out of your ears yet?"

"I'm afraid not, Shawn. The nurses won't let me have any cigarettes."

"I'll sneak some in for you," Shawn said.

Grandpa hugged him and laughed. "No, little one, you don't have to do that. Anyway, I don't even want them. Cigarettes are very bad for a person, Shawn. It's not good to smoke."

"But I like to see the smoke come out of your ears."

"So did your sister. Remember, Heather?"

Do I remember . . . *"How do you do it, Grandpa? Do it again. Take a puff and let the smoke come out of your ears. Oh, Grandpa, please tell me how you do it."*

How long did it take for me to realize that he held

the cigarette behind his head and let the smoke drift off to the sides? But I never told him I knew. I just let him go on believing that I believed. And no doubt he let me go on believing that he believed that I believed.

We talked about my mother and father's trip to the Caribbean, and my stay at Shani's house.

"You were there for *Shabbos*?" Grandpa asked.

"Not only was I there for *Shabbos*, but I even went to *shul* in the morning." I had said *shul*. Not *Temple*. Not *synagogue*. But *shul*. Grandpa didn't say anything, but a look of surprise mingled with happiness crossed his face.

Aunt Gloria decided to take Grandpa for a walk around the building. "Come on," she said, linking her arm in his, "I want you to take me on the grand tour."

"It's not so grand," he said, "but I'll be happy to take you."

"And I'll be happy to take you on a grand tour of the bathroom," I said to Shawn.

"I don't have to go."

"You don't have to now, but when we're on the highway you'll suddenly get the urge."

After the bathroom I bought Shawn a bag of Fritos, so he wouldn't complain about being hungry. With little kids you learn to anticipate.

The hardest part about visiting Grandpa was leaving him. Pity and guilt went home with me after each visit.

47

"We'll be by again next Sunday," Aunt Gloria told Grandpa. "Is there anything we can bring you?"

"Just yourselves," Grandpa said.

"I'll call you during the week," I said.

Grandpa bent down and Shawn threw his arms around his neck. "I'll call you too, Grandpa."

On the long drive home, Aunt Gloria kept Shawn entertained with her hinky pinks. "What do you call an angry father?" she asked him.

"What?" Shawn asked, his mouth full of Fritos.

"A mad dad."

He laughed his high-pitched laugh and sputtered wet Fritos crumbs.

"And what do you call an unhappy father?" Aunt Gloria continued.

"I give up."

"A sad dad."

"But Daddy, if Grandpa's out of danger I don't see why he can't come home with us. It would be better than having him stay there by himself."

"Don't you think I want that too, Heather? But it wouldn't work out. He needs special care—a special diet—and there's the kosher problem on top of that. It just wouldn't work out."

No matter. I convinced myself that in time everything *would* work out. In time Grandpa would become strong and well again. In time he'd go back to his own apartment and be able to take care of himself. In time.

"Hey, Shawn," I said. "I've got one for you. What do you call a glad grandfather?"

"What?" Shawn asked.

"A happy grandpappy," I said.

"It doesn't rhyme right," Shawn said.

5

Chanukah, the Festival of Lights, came out the following week. At our house, Chanukah is either celebrated to the hilt or totally ignored. Its significance—or lack of it—is in direct proportion to its proximity to Christmas. If the two holidays are more than a week apart, Chanukah goes by unnoticed. But if they coincide, then we go all out. I love it when they coincide. Because instead of getting just one gift, Shawn and I receive eight of them. One for each night of the holiday. All is bright and festive with holiday decorations on every door and window of our house, and our electric menorah wishes the entire world a Happy Chanukah.

Across the street, the Lipmans outshine all the rest of us with their eight-foot oil-burning menorah on their front lawn. When I first saw it, I thought the Ku Klux Klan was burning a cross in front of their house.

Last year on the eighth night of Chanukah, Shani and I had stood in amazement in front of the blazing menorah. I thought it was magnificent.

"It certainly is impressive," I had told Shani.

"I think it's showy and in poor taste," Shani had said. "Chanukah is a minor holiday. I just can't understand why people act as if it were the most important one on the Jewish calendar."

My Chanukah at the Greenwalds' was worlds apart from all the others. Every day after school, after my daily ritual of checking my house for burglars and the mail for postcards from Haiti, I went over to Shani's, where she and Mrs. Greenwald greeted me with samples of the potato pancakes that would be the main part of the night's dinner.

There was no electric menorah here. Every evening, before we ate, Mr. Greenwald lit Chanukah candles. Small spiral candles of red, yellow, blue, and green. We began with one candle on the first night, and ended up with eight candles on the last night. Eight candles plus the *shamas*—the service candle that's used to light all the others. The one that takes its place in the center of the menorah, higher than the rest.

"Go ahead and choose your colors, Shani," Mr. Greenwald said on the first night.

"Daddy, come on now," Shani said, obviously embarrassed and feeling the need to explain. "When I

51

was little, I always wanted to pick out the candles so I could choose whatever colors I wanted. I've been picking them out ever since."

She plucked a red candle from the box and put it on the menorah. "You can choose the *shamas*, Heather."

"Oh, goody, I'll take blue," I said, and we both giggled.

"We'd better raise the window shade a little higher," Mrs. Greenwald said. "We don't want a repeat of what happened a few years ago."

"We almost burned the kitchen down when the shade caught fire," Shani said.

Mr. Greenwald lit the candles and sang the prayers, and then we all sat down to the potato pancakes—or *latkes* as they called them. They were delicious topped with sour cream.

While I ate I watched the flames of the tiny candles flickering against the darkness of the window.

"They look so lonely, just the two of them," I said.

"They do now," Shani agreed. "But just wait until they're all lit. They're beautiful. You look at them and wish they'd never burn down."

After we ate they sang Chanukah songs. In Hebrew and in English. Mrs. Greenwald sang a song about a *dreidel*.

> I have a little *dreidel*
> I made it out of clay
> And when it's dry and ready
> Then *dreidel* I shall play.

"Actually I don't have a *dreidel* made out of clay, but I do have this one," she said, producing the tiny silver top with Hebrew letters on the four sides. "I've had it since I was about six years old."

"That old, huh?" Shani said. "Gee, Mom, it must be a real antique by now."

"Not quite, but it might well be considered a collector's item. You don't see many of these anymore. Most *dreidel*s are made out of plastic."

Shani started to sing, "I had a little *dreidel*, I made it out of plastic—" when Mr. Greenwald interrupted her.

"How about a game?"

He went into the kitchen and brought out a bag of nuts—walnuts, filberts, and almonds, still in their shells.

"You can play with anything," he said. "Pennies, candy, bubble gum. . . ."

"Heather and I once used marbles," Shani said.

I had played *dreidel* with Shani before, but from one year to the next I always forgot what the letters meant. While Mrs. Greenwald passed out all the nuts and put some in the center of the table for the pot, Mr. Greenwald explained.

"The letters stand for A Great Miracle Happened There, but for the game they have different meanings. We each take a turn spinning the *dreidel*. If it lands on this letter, *nun*, you get nothing. On *gimmel* you win the whole pot. *Hay* you get half, and *shin*, you put one in. Got it?"

"Got it."

53

We played *dreidel* every evening after dinner, and by the end of the week I knew the names of four Hebrew letters and won eighteen nuts—mostly filberts.

"Eighteen is a lucky number," Mrs. Greenwald said. "It stands for the Hebrew word *chai* (it rhymes with *eye* and you pronounce the *ch* like you're clearing your throat) and it means 'life.' "

"Like *l'chayim*?" I asked. "To life?"

"Exactly," she said, and I was very pleased with myself for getting the connection.

Mr. and Mrs. Greenwald then gave Shani and me our eighth Susan B. Anthony dollar. They had given us one dollar on each night of Chanukah. Chanukah *gelt* was what Mr. Greenwald called the coins. That's what Grandpa called them too. He always gave Shawn and me Chanukah *gelt* if we were lucky enough to see him during the holiday. Big silver dollars. How I remember those. I can barely remember the toys I got for Chanukah when I was small. But I'll never forget those big silver dollars he plucked out of the air. And when we went to visit him on Sunday, he kept producing shiny quarters from behind our ears.

Shani had vacation that whole week and she spent most of it with the synagogue youth group. Shoshana Katz was unanimously elected president and she immediately went to work planning for the year's activities, which included such long-range plans as winter retreats, summer retreats, spring retreats, and fall retreats.

"However," said Shani, "she hasn't the slightest idea where we're retreating to."

Our first outing was the scavenger hunt that Heshy had mentioned. On Saturday night we rode to Newark Airport in a chartered bus. There were about twenty kids plus the group adviser, Kevin Cornfield, a heavyset bearded guy in his twenties.

It seemed strange to see all the boys wearing their skullcaps. After all, they weren't even in a synagogue. I could imagine my mother's reaction if she were here—*"Wearing them on a bus to the airport, for God's sake"*—and I felt uncomfortable.

I knew by that time that a skullcap was not called a skullcap. It was called a *kipa* (kee pa). Most of them were small knitted ones that had the boys' names on in Hebrew or English. Heshy was one of the few kids who didn't have a name on his, and I couldn't help thinking how one day I would crochet one for him and he would say, *"Oh, thank you, Heather darling. I have always wanted a* kipa *with my name on it. It must have taken you a very long time to do this."*

And I would say, *"Not really, Heshy dear. I've had a lot of practice crocheting pot holders in Girl Scouts. The name was a little tricky, though."*

No, that whole scene was very unlikely. How could I ever get serious about a boy who wore one of those things?

We split up into four groups and sat in different parts of the bus to plan strategy. I sat in the back with Shani, Heshy, Shoshana, and Donald Gluck, who was tall and thin and blinking like mad because he was trying to get used to his contact lenses.

"I fell in love with Donald in kindergarten," Shani whispered to me. "He had the biggest box of crayons in the whole class."

"I guess that's as good a reason as any," I said.

"There was another reason too."

"He shared his milk and cookies with you?"

"No. I realized that if I married him I wouldn't have to change my initials. But that wasn't until third grade."

Shoshana was itching to get started with the hunt. "Let's study the list right now so we won't have to waste time in the airport," she said. She read aloud from the list each group was given.

> foreign stamps (not licked)
> foreign coins (not Canadian)
> air-sickness bag (not used)
> American Airlines flight attendant pin
> count number of steps on escalator . . .

"Heshy," she said—and she was practically sitting on his lap—"why don't you and I get the stamps and coins while Shani, Heather, and Donald count the steps on the escalator?"

"Uh . . . well . . . I think we'd all better stick together. We don't want anyone getting lost. And we've got to take care of old Donald here. He can't see too well these days." He gave old Donald a punch in the arm.

"I'll be okay," Donald said, his eyes red and tearing. "I have to force myself to get used to them. It's only been a few days."

When the bus pulled up in front of the airport, Kevin Cornfield announced, "I'm not sure if scavenger hunts are allowed here, so don't make it obvious. And we meet back here at ten sharp."

"Synchronize your watches," some kid in front of the bus hollered out, and we all got off.

Once inside the airport I immediately spotted a group of people who looked foreign. They wore flowing green robes with wide sleeves.

"Over there," I said, and glanced in the group's direction. "The ones with the flowers."

"Great," Heshy said. "Let's go."

"Hurry," Shoshana said, "let's get to them before the others do."

"No," Shani said, and gently pulled her back. "We need you to count escalator steps."

"But we have to stay together."

"Your idea to split up was better."

Heshy and I left Shoshana with her mouth open and headed toward the foreigners.

"It was really quick of you to spot them like that," Heshy said on the way over. "I wonder where they're from."

"Probably some Far Eastern country. India maybe." Or was India in the Near East, or the Middle East?

We approached a tall, thin man, who like all the

57

others with him was bald, with just one braid sticking out of the middle of his head. He didn't look the least bit Indian.

"Excuse me," Heshy said very slowly, "but do you have a coin from your country? Just a small coin?" He was careful to enunciate each syllable so the man would understand him.

"Certainly," the man said, and reached into the pocket of his flowing green robe. He came out with a small copper coin with Abraham Lincoln stamped on it.

"This is a penny," Heshy said, staring at the coin.

"Yes it is. Won't you join us?"

"Join you?" I asked. Was he inviting us to India?

"Join us and come to the true worship of God. We are at the dawn of a new era. Let us bring a spiritual light into your dark, confused world."

"I think we have to go now," Heshy said.

"Yours is a crumbling civilization. Get out of the shambles."

We turned to leave.

". . . Out of the material clutches . . . onto a plane of spiritual understanding."

"Let's get out of here," said Heshy, grabbing my hand.

". . . Buy a flower. . . ."

We found Shani, Donald, and Shoshana crawling on the floor near the escalator.

"What are you all doing down there?" I asked.

Shani looked up and brushed the hair away from her eyes. "Did you find the foreigners?"

"They were strange," Heshy said, "but they weren't foreign. What's going on?"

Shani stood up and dusted herself off. "It's a long story. First we put little pieces of paper in the grooves of one of the steps to mark the place. But all the paper kept falling out. Then Donald decided to pop his lenses out so he could wear glasses and see better, but he lost one of the lenses, and now we're trying to find it."

We spent the rest of the evening on the floor looking for Donald's lens. At about nine forty-five Donald found it. Up his eyelid. We ended the evening at an Israeli restaurant, eating what could have been our first prize: falafel.

I went to see Grandpa early on Sunday, and in the afternoon, Shani's mother and father drove us into New York City to a kosher Chinese retaurant. Our Chinese waiter wore a *kipa* and served us kosher moo goo gai pan. Then we went to see a special photo exhibit at The Jewish Museum.

"It's called 'Another Time, Another Place,' " Mr. Greenwald said. "And it's supposed to be pretty good."

I didn't even know there was a Jewish museum, and when I went through it I couldn't help but marvel at all these ancient Torah scrolls and prayer books and menorahs and *kiddush* cups. And there were the most magnificent Torah mantles with silver and gold embroidery.

One of the Torahs had been rescued from the Nazis. It had been hidden away in a warehouse somewhere and sent to the museum after the war.

"This is fantastic," I said to Shani. "I never knew such a place existed."

And if I was inspired by the words of yesterday's Jews, I was even more inspired by the photographs of those who had lived a hundred years ago or so. Maybe it's because I find it hard to believe that people actually lived before me. And photographs like these were proof that there did exist a time before this time.

There were photographs taken by Kipnis and Rotenberg that showed seventeenth- and eighteenth-century wooden synagogues, Jewish children playing on cobblestone streets, Jewish marketplaces, and Ezrielke, the *Shabbos Klopper*.

"The *Shabbos Klopper* was the one who went around knocking on shutters to let people know that the Sabbath was about to begin," Mrs. Greenwald explained. And looking at the photograph again, I could almost hear him knocking on that shutter.

Mr. Greenwald summed up the whole museum experience by saying, "We have been around a long time. Whenever I come here, I feel such a sense of belonging."

I knew what he meant. I felt it too. A link with the past. I would have to come back again—with Grandpa. And maybe we could bring Shawn along. To show him where he came from. For a moment I even thought of bringing my mother here too. She probably didn't know this place existed either. But if she knew about it, would she even care?

After I had been at the Greenwalds' for a couple of weeks, I began worrying about my mother and father. As yet I had not heard a word from them. At first I was just disappointed at not finding anything in the mailbox. But then I really began to worry. Especially at night.

There's something about the night that's conducive to worrying. Worries and problems that seem minor during the day are magnified and blown completely out of proportion at night. So, lying in bed one night, I knew why I hadn't heard from my parents. Their ship had sunk. What else could have happened? The authorities tried to contact me but didn't know where I could be reached. How could they know I was staying at Shani's house? Shawn and I were orphans and we'd have to go live with Aunt Gloria and eat health foods.

Shani heard me tossing and turning. I was making the whole bunk bed squeak.

"Are you having trouble sleeping?" Shani asked softly.

"Yes. A little. I've been thinking about my mother and father. I haven't heard from them yet. Shani . . . do you think . . . could the ship have . . ."

"Of course not. Your mother and father are okay. The mail is just slow. That's all. And nothing happened to the ship. An ocean liner doesn't go under without people hearing about it. Imagine the *Titanic* sinking and nobody knowing."

"You're right, of course. Thanks, Shani," I said, and curled up under the blanket.

6

A postcard came a few days later. A picture of the S.S. *Rotterdam* was on one side of it, and my mother's handwriting was on the other. I was so thrilled and relieved that I read the card four times.

Heather dear,
   We're on the way to Jamaica. The sea is calm, the weather is beautiful, and your father is seasick. Lots of interesting people here. Should get some good story ideas. I've even come up with a title, "I Fell in Love with a Stowaway." What do you think? We miss you and hope you're not having trouble adjusting. Take care of yourself.
                    Love and kisses from us both,
                    Mom

Trouble adjusting? Actually, I was surprising my-self by adjusting so well. And Mom, if you only knew that, you would have swum all the way back to New Jersey to rescue me.

Even Shani noticed how well I was adjusting. "I told you you'd learn where everything is," she said one night when we were setting the table. It had be-come second nature now for me to reach for the cor-rect dishes and silverware whenever I set the table or went to get myself something to eat. It was no big thing once I got used to it.

"And do you realize," Shani went on, "you never once asked for milk when we were eating meat?"

"To tell you the truth, I never even thought of having meat and milk together since I've been here. Except for that first night. And I'd rather forget all about that."

Audrey and Roseann were getting impatient with me.

"Why can't you go bowling with us?" Roseann asked after school on the third Friday of my stay with Shani. "It's not your first night there anymore."

"It still wouldn't be right," I said.

"Come on," Audrey urged. "We'll show you the boys who keep trying to pick us up."

"It looks like you're having better luck without me."

"We already told you. They're horrendous."

"I'm sorry, but I really can't go. It would be dis-respectful to leave. Friday nights mean a lot to the

Greenwalds." I didn't tell them that I was beginning to look forward to Friday nights too.

We parted at the corner and I ran home to check the mail and to change into a fresh sweater and my only skirt. I had already worn it four times.

I guess Shani's fondness for jewelry was contagious. I searched through my jewelry box and found a small gold chain necklace with a tiny Jewish star dangling from it. Grandma Hannah had given it to me shortly before she died. And though I hadn't worn it in ages, I very much wanted to wear it now. I put the necklace on—surprisingly it still fit around my neck—and ran over to Shani's.

There was the usual frantic rush to get everything done before sunset; the last-minute cooking and cleaning.

"Will someone please run the vacuum and finish up the table?" Mrs. Greenwald called from the kitchen.

"I'll do the table," I said to Shani. "I can always vacuum at home."

I put out the wineglasses and set the two loaves of challah on the table. Then I opened the door to the buffet and reached for the two pairs of candleholders that Shani and her mother would be using that night. I saw a third pair and was tempted to take it out. For a brief moment I saw myself lighting the Sabbath candles too. But I thought of my mother. She would never light candles. Not even when my grandfather asked her that one time when we visited him on a Friday evening. "No, Pa, I'd rather not," she had

64

said. I remember now how much I had wanted to light the candles for him. But I didn't dare ask. Not with my mother there. So Grandpa had to light them himself.

I set the two pairs of candleholders on the table and closed the door.

I enjoyed the evening: the lighted candles, the food, the singing, the warmth that was all around me.

"You're probably anxious to get back home and back to your usual routine," Mrs. Greenwald commented to me.

I shrugged. "I'm not so sure," I said. "It's been very nice here."

In the morning I woke up before Shani. I tapped her on the shoulder.

"Wake up," I said. "We'll be late for services."

"It's too cold," she said, pulling the blanket up over her head.

"Come on, Shani, let's go."

Her only answer was a groan.

"You mean I got dressed for nothing?"

She peeked out from under the blanket. "You really *are* dressed, aren't you?"

"Sure. I'm all ready."

"Okay," she said, crawling out of bed. "In that case I'll go with you. But it's crazy, you know, *you* dragging *me* to *shul*."

"I know it is. But it's all your fault for getting me into the habit of going." I neglected to mention that I also wanted to see Heshy.

While Shani was getting dressed, I thought about

the new clothes I'd need for Saturdays at the synagogue. I couldn't wear the same skirt over and over again.

"A few more skirts and tops," I said. "That's what I need."

"For what?" Shani asked, pulling a sweater over her head.

"For services. Except for this one skirt all I have are jeans."

Shani picked up a brush and gave her hair a few light strokes. "By the time you get around to buying them, you won't be needing them anymore."

"Why would you say that?"

"Heather," she said, putting down her hairbrush, "once you leave here and you're home doing your usual things, you won't be giving any thought to going to services."

"I guess you're right, Shani. But I should get some new things anyway, just in case I decide to go with you once in a while."

Later in the afternoon, after services and lunch, Shani and I met with Kevin Cornfield and the rest of the kids. I spent an afternoon with them the week before, and I looked forward to going. Kevin led some pretty interesting discussions about things like assimilation and intermarriage and Jews in the world situation. It was kind of funny to see the same kids who one week earlier were counting escalator steps, now talking about Israel and their plans to work and study there after graduation.

"I'd like to go to the *ulpan*," Heshy was saying. He

seemed to be looking straight at me when he said that, and I thought he deserved some sort of response.

"Sounds good," I said, even though I didn't have the slightest idea what the *ulpan* was. I thought maybe it was a place to visit. A famous tourist attraction or something. Maybe Heshy and I could go there together. We could travel to the *ulpan* and take pictures.

"Where's the *ulpan*?" I asked Shani in a whisper.

"The *ulpan* is an intensive course in Hebrew," she said.

"Oh."

"When you come out of it you can speak like a sabra."

Back at the house I told Shani that I'd like to go to the *ulpan* too, one day, and learn some Hebrew. That remark plus the way I totally ignored the ringing telephone a few minutes later caused her to say, "You know, Heather, I think you're undergoing some sort of metamorphosis or something."

Metamorphosis. That was a good word for what was happening to me. But I couldn't help it. And I couldn't understand it either. What was going on, anyway? None of this was working out the way it was supposed to. I was supposed to be feeling terribly uncomfortable here, missing my bacon and Twinkies, desperately feeling the need to escape to Aunt Gloria's. I was here only because my father and Nate were such old friends. In January I would go home and my mother and I could have a good laugh over all this Jewishness, and my mother could tell my father, "See, I told you so." Instead I was metamorphosing. Maybe it was just a temporary condition and I would go into remission. But I found myself metamorphosing when I least expected to.

Take the lunches with Audrey and Roseann, for instance.

The lunches in the school cafeteria were never anything to brag about. But some of their specialties, like the sloppy joes, were downright inedible. Horrendous, as Audrey puts it. One day when the cafeteria featured Swiss steak, which was really cardboard soaked in cold gravy, we went to The Hangout, a little place across the street.

The Hangout had been the prize-winning name in the Name This Restaurant contest that took place when the eating establishment changed ownership at the start of the school year. None of us could think of any names, except for Roseann who wanted to call it Roseann's. But if they were to hold the same contest today we could come up with any number of entries: Heartburn Haven, Grease 'n Guk, Down in the Dumps.

There wasn't much of a selection there, so we usually ordered hamburgers and malts. I was the last one to order.

"I'll have a hamburger and a Coke." I said *Coke* automatically, without thinking.

"Coke?" Audrey and Roseann looked at me as if I had said something obscene.

"Sure," I said. "Why not?"

"Because you always get a malt with your burger," Roseann answered.

Meat and milk together? I couldn't.

"I know . . . but . . . I'm on a diet."

"Why would you be on a diet? You're so skinny."

I was not skinny. Flat-chested, yes. And spindly-legged. But not skinny. And a malt wasn't going to help any.

"There are all kinds of diets," I said. "Not all have to do with gaining or losing weight."

"Diet, huh?" Audrey said. She looked up at the waitress who was still standing there, taking it all in. "Maybe I'll skip the French fries." The waitress crossed out *French fries*.

"Hey, wait a minute," Audrey said as an after-thought, "I'm not on a diet. I think I'll have the fries after all."

The waitress wrote *French fries* on her pad again. She stood there, waiting some more and tapping her pencil on her pad.

"Have we all decided what we're getting?" she asked.

"Sure," I said. "I'll have the Coke and she'll have the fries."

I drank the Coke and left the hamburger. I couldn't even bring myself to take one bite out of it. I wished The Hangout was a kosher restaurant and the hamburger was a kosher hamburger. I thought about my mother, and I felt guilty about the wish. This was silly. Who cared if the hamburger was kosher or not? I gave it to Roseann.

I must have gone off the deep end the weekend of the *Shabbaton.* Something must have snapped. A few days before my winter vacation, Shani's freshman class held a weekend of religious and social activities at the school. I was looking forward to it because I knew lots of the kids who would be there. Most of the kids I met with on Saturdays also went to the Hebrew high school.

I borrowed another one of Shani's skirts and packed a few things for the night and next day, because we would be sleeping over.

"It feels funny taking pajamas to school," Shani said as she handed me Beth's sleeping bag. "I mean, who ever heard of sleeping in school?"

"I get some of my best sleeping done in school," I said. "Especially during Western Civilization."

"My best time is in biology, during fermentation. Which necklace should I wear? My English Shani or my Hebrew Shani?"

"Your Hebrew, definitely." I was still wearing my grandmother's star.

"Why definitely?"

"It fits the occasion."

"I was hoping you'd say that," she said, and sprayed me with her Wind Song. I sprayed her back with Calvin Klein.

Mrs. Greenwald forced us to wear our boots and bundle up in heavy winter coats, even though Mr. Greenwald was driving us to the school, which was less than a mile away.

"The girls will be sleeping on the first floor and the

boys will be up on the second floor," Shani said when we went into the building.

"Oh, rats. You mean it's not going to be coed?"

"Are you kidding? I'm surprised they agreed to go this far. But you can be sure they'll have plenty of chaperones around. Let's go find us a nice cozy little corner."

We made our way through the corridor, stepping over sleeping bags, pillows and blankets, and bodies. We claimed squatters' rights at the very end of the corridor and then went off to the lunchroom where the dinner was to be held. Shani stood frozen in the doorway.

"They've transformed this place. Just look at it."

The room was dimly lit, and there were long tables set with white cloths and blue Star of David centerpieces. Up close you could see the plates that looked like china were really plastic, and so were the glasses that looked like crystal. Along one wall was another long table with about twenty-five pairs of brass-colored candleholders with white candles.

"I just can't believe it," Shani said. "This afternoon a lunchroom. Tonight . . . a banquet hall."

"Who gets to light all those candles?" I asked.

"Any girl who wants to. Would you like to light a pair?"

"Who, me? I wouldn't even know how."

"I'll help you. There's nothing to it. You've seen it done lots of times."

"But what prayer do you say when you cover your eyes?"

"I'll say it so you can hear—and in English. All you have to do is say it with me. Come on. They're going up now."

"I don't know, Shani. I don't think . . ."

"It'll be okay. Come on."

I walked over to the table, certain that everyone's eyes were on me, certain that everyone knew that the only candles I had ever lit before were birthday candles. She doesn't know the prayer, they were saying. Heather Hopkowitz doesn't know the prayer.

The first step was easy. I lit the match. Then the candles. I made the circular motion above the flames, just as the others were doing. Just as Grandma Hannah had done so long ago. I held my hands over my eyes, just as the others were doing. And Grandma Hannah. It was as if she and I were both there lighting candles together. Or maybe she and I had become one in the same.

Shani began the prayer. And I said it with her.

> Blessed art Thou, O Lord our God,
> King of the Universe
> Who has sanctified us with
>   His commandments
> and commanded us to kindle
>   the Sabbath lights.

I heard the greeting, *Shabbat Shalom*, and opened my eyes. The sight was magnificent. All those lighted candles. I couldn't take my eyes off them. My first

72

pair of *Shabbos* candles. I felt wonderful. As if I were away for a long time and was coming back.

"You can have them," Shani said.

"Have them?"

"The candleholders. You can keep them. They'll remain on the table until after *Shabbos*. And then you can take a pair home."

"Are you sure, Shani? Because I'd really like that."

"I'm sure," she said.

"But it's got to be this very same pair."

"It will be," she said. "Let's go to services."

The school has its own synagogue right in the building. A small synagogue, but very lovely—even if the boys and girls do sit separately here too. Shani and I waved to Heshy and Donald across the room.

The services were beautiful that night. Outside there was cold and darkness, and branches scratched at the windows as if they were trying to get inside where it was warm and bright, where soft melodies filled the air. I wished I knew the Hebrew words so I could sing along with everyone.

One of the prayers, *Lechah Dodi,* was so pretty, I found myself reading the translation to see what it meant.

> Come, my friend, to meet the bride;
> Let us welcome the Sabbath.

I nudged Shani and interrupted her singing. "I didn't know the Sabbath was referred to as a bride."

"It is," she said. "A beautiful, radiant bride."

How I wished I knew those words.

When the services were over and we started walking toward the dining hall, someone began a new song, which was soon taken up by more and more voices. They sang, like one sweet voice, a song even more beautiful than any of the others. And as I listened, my spirit seemed to be lifted right out of me, up to the highest place.

"Tell me what they're singing now," I begged Shani.

"That's *'Shabbos Ha-Malkah,'* about going to meet the Sabbath queen."

How lovely, I thought. The Sabbath was radiant and beautiful. Like a bride, like a queen.

The singing subsided as we entered the dining hall, and I gently floated down to earth. I knew I was on earth again when Shani and I met up with Heshy and Donald. I was surprised to see Donald wearing glasses. I almost didn't recognize him.

Shani seemed surprised to see him in glasses too. "What happened to your contacts?" she asked.

"I wanted to have a good time tonight," he said, "so I decided to wait until Sunday to suffer."

"Would you girls consider sitting with us?" Heshy asked.

"I don't know, Shani, what do you think? Would it spoil our image to be seen with them?"

"Well, it might, but let's do it anyway. After all, if we don't sit with them, who will?"

"Thank you," Heshy said. "That's very kind. Right this way. We're sitting with the president."

Shoshana Katz was already at the table, warming up Heshy's seat with her hand. She gave the seat a pat and motioned for him to sit down. Heshy either didn't see, or ignored her signal, and slipped in between Shani and me. Scott Applebaum came over and sat down next to Shoshana. He was immediately followed by Sunny Margolis.

The name Sunny conjures up visions of a sun-tanned girl with a sunny personality and sun-streaked hair blowing in the wind. She's on TV, drinking Coke and Pepsi and Dr Pepper. Sunny Margolis was pale, she had black hair, and her personality was about as sunny as a wet towel.

After everyone was seated, the principal recited the *kiddush* over the Kedem grape juice.

"I wonder what he really has in that glass of his," Scott Applebaum said.

"Grape juice. Like the rest of us," said Sunny Margolis.

"I was just kidding."

"Oh."

We had chopped liver, chicken soup, roast chicken, and all those side dishes that I had eaten before at Shani's house. And I, Heather Hopkowitz, knew the names of all of them. I couldn't wait for someone to ask me to pass the *farfel* or *tzimmes* or *kasha varnishkes* so I could show how knowledgeable I was.

75

"This stuff is great," Heshy said. "Why can't Fanny cook like this all the time?"

"This doesn't taste like Fanny's cooking," Donald said.

"The dinner's catered," said Sunny with a mouth full of farfel.

Throughout the meal, in between courses we sang *zemirot*. Sabbath songs. We sang between the chopped liver and the chicken soup, we sang between the chicken and the dessert. I knew lots of melodies from the Friday nights with Shani, and I even knew some of the words. So there I was, eating kosher food, singing Hebrew songs, and feeling very Jewish, when a bunch of kids ran up to do some Hebrew dancing. Another bunch joined them, including Heshy, Donald, Shoshana, Scott, Sunny, and Shani. Shani ran off and came back a second later to retrieve me—like a forgotten package.

"Come on, Heather."

"No, Shani. I can't."

"Sure you can."

"Don't force me."

"I'm forcing you. Come on. Just follow everyone else."

We broke into the dancing circle and joined hands. Around and around we went, singing and dancing, my feet not knowing where they were going. Slowly at first, and then faster and faster we danced, until I was leaping and flying with the rest of them. And if I couldn't catch on to all the steps, it didn't matter.

There was so much happy confusion. Fast dances, slow dances, circles within circles. We danced like that, danced and sang until it was almost midnight.

"I'll never be able to sleep tonight," I said to Shani from my sleeping bag. "I'm still dancing around inside."

"Me too," she said.

Some falsetto voices called a greeting from the stairway. "Yoo hoo, girls, good night." We turned around and saw these boys in pajamas waving from the steps. All of us broke into giggles. And giggling is the last thing I remember doing before I fell asleep.

It was a crazy kind of sleep that I fell into. I kept going in and out of dreams. Maybe it was because of the dancing. I had this one weird dream about my mother, swimming. She was swimming all the way back to New Jersey to rescue me. And she was calling to me.

"I'm coming, Heather. Don't go any further. I'm coming."

In the morning I took that dream with me to services. And as I looked out the window, at the bare trees and the falling snow, I thought about my mother. She was coming to rescue me. From what? From the Sabbath Bride and Sabbath Queen? From the beautiful melodies that were becoming such a part of me? From the humming and chanting that filled the synagogue each Saturday, just as it was filling the synagogue this morning?

Oh, Mom, I'm sorry. I didn't mean for all this to happen. Please try to understand.

The Torah was being placed back in the ark. I looked down at my *siddur,* and found the passage they were singing from.

> Forsake not my Torah.
> It is a tree of life to those who
>   take hold of it.
> And happy are those who support it.
> Its ways are ways of pleasantness,
> And all its paths are peace.

A tree of life to those who take hold of it. I turned those words over and over in my mind all during the lunch that followed the services.

"Aren't you coming?" Shani was beckoning to me. "Don't you want to dance with us?"

"Yes, Shani, I do." Yes, yes, I want to be a part of all this. And I got up and danced and sang with everyone.

7

Mr. Greenwald came for us that night about eleven. I packed my things and went to get what I could not forget. The candleholders were on the table waiting where I had left them, and I brought them back with me to Shani's house.

I sat cross-legged on the floor in Shani's room and chopped away at the candle wax with a bobby pin. I laughed to myself and shook my head. It was ironic. All these years—I was feeling sorry for Shani. The poor kid couldn't go anyplace or do anything good on Saturdays. She couldn't have any fun like the rest of us. The poor kid. I laughed again, a little louder this time. Shani looked at me and my eyes held hers.

"I never knew," I said. "I never understood about *Shabbos*. I always thought . . ."

"That it was solemn and grim? Lots of people think that. People who don't understand. Someone once asked me if I could have visitors on Saturday. As if I were in seclusion or something."

"I never thought of it as solemn or grim. Just kind of dull for you. Like you couldn't wait for Saturday to be over so you could get back to living. But it's not like that at all. There's something special . . . a feeling . . . a spirit. I can't quite explain it. It's just so different from the rest of the week."

"The difference is what makes it special," Shani said. "It's a lot more than just a day of rest."

"Rest? I'm exhausted. And my aunt's picking me up early tomorrow so we can go see my grandfather before I go to stay with her."

"Maybe you can come back by Friday," Shani said. "Then we can spend *Shabbos* together."

"Great. I'd like that." I got up from the floor and went over to put the candleholders on Shani's dresser. No use in taking them with me to Aunt Gloria's, I thought. They would only bring up questions.

But I had a question that needed bringing up. I didn't even look at Shani when I asked it.

"Shani . . . is it hard . . . is it hard to be observant?"

She took my place on the floor, crossed her legs, and fingered her Shani necklace. She looked like she was doing yoga. Thinking, concentrating, getting ready to contemplate her navel.

"I never thought of it as being hard. It's just a way of life. It's the only way I've ever known. I can't

80

imagine living any other way. I don't know what else to tell you, Heather."

"Shani, you'll think I'm crazy. And I know my mother and father will put me in therapy. But I'm thinking of converting—to Orthodoxy. At least I think I'd like to give it a try."

Shani flashed me the same kind of look my grandfather gave me when I told him I went to *shul*. These words would not bring such delight to Abbey and Harvey Hopkowitz. Well, maybe Harvey wouldn't mind too much. How is it that the same thing can mean so many different things to different people?

"Of course I don't think you're crazy. And you're not the only one who's come to that decision, you know. I know a few other kids who have decided to become observant. There's Scott Applebaum, for instance."

"Scott Applebaum? Are you serious?"

"Sure. He had a secret Bar Mitzvah."

A secret Bar Mitzvah. I couldn't believe such a thing. It sounded like the title of one of my mother's confession stories. "I Didn't Know about My Son's Secret Bar Mitzvah."

"Why would his Bar Mitzvah have to be a secret?"

"His parents were dead set against it."

"Unbelievable. Even my mother and father wouldn't go that far. They'll probably have some real big splash for Shawn when it's his time."

"Just the same, Scott wanted to become Bar Mitzvah and his parents wouldn't hear of it. So some friends of his taught him the blessings. He became

Bar Mitzvah right in our *shul* and we were his family."

"That's sad," I said.

"It sure is. He belongs to the youth group and his parents don't like it. He wants to go to the Hebrew high school and they won't let him. He was just visiting there this weekend. Same as you. It's really a shame too, because he's very sincere about becoming a practicing Jew."

A practicing Jew. Yes. That's what I would become. I would bring a spiritual light into my dark, confused world. I turned around and looked at myself in the mirror. Almost a whole month of kosher food and it didn't do a thing for my complexion. Maybe it takes more than a month, I thought. No matter. I had already made up my mind. I would move onto a plane of spiritual understanding. I would trade my Temple in for a *shul*. The decision was made. It was final and irrevocable. And even if my mother and father would have rushed in on me that very moment, it would have been too late.

8

Aunt Gloria didn't realize she had a complete stranger staying in her home. She thought I was the same old Heather Hopkowitz.

"I apologize for my empty freezer," she said over our Sunday dinner of rice balls and seaweed. "But I just didn't get a chance to stock up on steaks and hamburger for you. Shawn's eating the last bit of meat in the house."

I eyed Shawn's hamburger and resisted the urge to snatch it out from under his nose. "Oh, I don't mind, Aunt Gloria. Really. These rice balls are very interesting."

"You can have a bite," Shawn said, pushing the juicy hamburger into my face. The aroma hung in the air and ketchup was oozing out of the roll. I gently pushed it away.

"No thanks, honey."

"Go on, take a bite." He stuck the hamburger back under my nose.

"Really, Shawn, I don't want any. You eat it. Okay?"

He just shrugged and started stuffing his mouth.

"It's not that I've given up meat completely," Aunt Gloria said, taking another rice ball, "but I've been eating less and less of it lately, and I've been feeling so much better. More get-up-and-go. More zip. But first thing tomorrow we'll go out and get whatever you'd like."

"You know, Aunt Gloria, I've been thinking. Why don't you just get a few things for Shawn? I'd kind of like to try some of your natural foods while I'm here. They might be good for a change. I think I'd like to skip meat completely."

"Heather, that's wonderful," Aunt Gloria said, flashing her brown and blue eyes. "I'm really happy to hear that. You can't imagine what variety there is and how tasty everything will be. Why, I'll open up a whole new world for you. Wait and see. We'll have avocado burgers, grain burgers, and my specialty, squash soufflé. Just for starters."

"That's great," I said. "Really great." I imagined myself eating squash soufflé and gulped down some water to take the taste away.

After dinner we watched TV and munched un-salted soybeans from Back to Nature. Then Aunt

84

Gloria made up the couch for Shawn and the floor for me.

"Can I sleep on the floor with you?" Shawn asked.

I lifted the blanket for him. "Sure. Come on in."

"Can my panda sleep with you too?"

"Okay, it's a big floor."

He giggled and he and Panda curled up next to me.

We spent the next few days helping out at the health food store, serving and drinking carrot juice and banana smoothies. My breakfasts during the week consisted of sprout omelets and granola, and while Shawn ate lamb chops for dinner, I had steamed zucchini with eggplant parmigiana and dreamed of chopped liver and rib roasts and Friday night dinner with Shani.

"Are you sure you can't stay for the weekend?" Aunt Gloria asked. "I thought we'd take in a movie Saturday afternoon."

"A Walt Disney one," Shawn said.

"A new Walt Disney?" I asked Aunt Gloria.

"The same Walt Disney," she said, and heaved a sigh.

"It figures," I said. Shawn can see the same movie ten times and never get tired of it. It's the same way with a book he likes. He loves to hear the story over and over again, long after he's learned the words by heart.

"I'd really like to join you, Aunt Gloria. But I promised Shani I'd be back by Friday."

I had Aunt Gloria drive me back on Thursday because she didn't think she could get me to Shani's until late Friday. And I certainly didn't want to violate my first Sabbath as a sincere practicing Jew.

I knew something was wrong the minute I saw Shani. I had made one of my disgusting faces in front of the peephole—I had my nose angled so Shani could look up my nostrils—but when she opened the door she wasn't laughing. She managed a faint smile.

"Hi, Heather. I was hoping it would be you."

"What's the matter, Shani? You don't look right."

"Come on in and I'll tell you about it," she said, leading the way into the living room. I sat down on the sofa and waited for her to say something.

"It's about Mr. Teitlebaum," she began. "He died yesterday."

"Mr. Teitlebaum? It can't be. We just saw him in *shul* on Saturday. He was passing out candy and joking around with everyone."

"I know. I couldn't believe it either. But it happened just after he ate lunch. He was sitting in a chair reading the paper, and he fell asleep. That was it. He never woke up. The funeral was just a couple of hours ago. I'm still shaky."

I felt a chill come over me and shivered. "I feel shaky too," I said, "and I wasn't even at the funeral."

"The family is sitting *shiva* at the Teitlebaums' house. We're going there tonight . . . if you want to come."

Shiva. The seven-day mourning period that Jews observe when a close relative dies. I have hazy memories of the time Grandma Hannah died and my father and Grandpa sat *shiva.* My mother and I went back and forth from our house to Grandpa's, but my father stayed there for the entire seven days.

"Of course I'll come, Shani. Just stick close to me."

Nobody knocked or rang the bell. Mr. Greenwald just opened the door and we walked right in. There were quite a few people already there. Some were sitting and some were standing around, talking quietly.

Mrs. Teitlebaum was sitting on a piano bench. Like Mr. Teitlebaum, she too was small and gray-haired. But that night she looked smaller and grayer than usual. She was in her stockinged feet, as were the much younger man and woman sitting next to her. A son and daughter, Shani told me.

Mr. and Mrs Greenwald went over to them and took their hands, and they all just kind of nodded to one another. Then they started talking. Shani went along with them and motioned for me to follow. But I didn't want to. I didn't really know Mrs. Teitlebaum. And I didn't know what in the world I could say to her. So I found a chair and sat down. After a few minutes Shani came and sat down next to me. We talked for a while and sometimes when we weren't speaking, I just looked around the room, at the memorial candle flickering in a yellow cylinder lamp, and at the dining room mirror, draped with a white cloth.

During the hour that we stayed there, people came and people left. And as they left they tried to offer words of comfort. "May you know no more sorrow," or as Mr. and Mrs Greenwald said, "May God comfort you among all the mourners of Zion and Jerusalem."

Everyone missed Mr. Teitlebaum at services on Saturday. Especially the little kids, who couldn't quite understand why he wasn't there. Somehow it wasn't the same without the candy man.

9

Welcome home! We hung up signs all around the house.

> We couldn't wait-i
> till you came back from Haiti.
>
> By jimini
> you're home from Bimini.

Shawn drew smiling faces and pictures of a man and woman who were supposed to be our mother and father, and by afternoon we had signs on the front door, the windows, and all over the entranceway that leads into the living room.

Aunt Gloria dusted the furniture, and Shawn kept

running back and forth to the window every time he heard a car passing.

"They're here, they're here!" he shouted, jumping up and down.

"That's what you said the last time," I told him. But when I looked out the window, I saw my mother and father getting out of a taxi.

"They really *are* here!" I shouted to Aunt Gloria, and the three of us grabbed our coats and ran outside.

When my father saw us he dropped the suitcases and spread out his arms. Shawn and I ran right into them.

"I can't believe you're home," I shouted and went from him to my mother and back and forth again. There was such a jumble of Welcome Home's and Good To Be Back's that my mother began to shiver from the cold, and said, "It's freezing out here. Let's finish this inside."

"A great welcome home," my father said when he saw all the signs in the doorway. His smile widened when he passed

> To Papa and Mama,
> home from the Bahama(s)

"This is the best part about being away," my mother said, and she hugged Shawn and me again.

When they took their coats off I could see how beautiful they looked in their summery tans. It was as if they had brought some of the Caribbean sun to the cold New Jersey winter.

Shawn stood there, looking, waiting, asking with his eyes, "What did you bring me?"

My mother read his eyes and answered them with a sailboat made out of seashells, and he immediately held the whole boat to his ear so he could hear the ocean. For me they brought a musical jewelry box that played the theme from *Swan Lake*, and for both of us, T-shirts that said: My Parents Went on a Caribbean Cruise and All I Got Was This Lousy T-shirt.

My mother handed me a small paper bag with a small package inside. "An extra bonus for you, Heather."

I opened up the bag and looked inside. "Of all things. Twinkies. I haven't had one of these in ages." I tried to look thrilled.

"That's what I thought," my mother said.

"What about me?" Shawn asked.

"We'll share," I said. Then I whispered to him, "You can have both of them."

My mother took out perfumes, linen, and jewelry that she brought back for herself and Aunt Gloria. Things that neither of them needed, but things she couldn't resist because they were duty-free and such bargains. One of the bottles of perfume would be for Shani, she said, and a linen tablecloth was for the Greenwalds. I thought of how nice it would look on their Sabbath table.

"Let's celebrate," my father said. "How about all of us going to some swanky place for dinner?"

"Count me out," Aunt Gloria said. "I've really got to get back home."

I guess after a month of baby-sitting, Aunt Gloria needed some time to herself.

My father chose a fancy steak house with a lot of atmosphere. Low lighting and soft music. We'd been there before and their steaks are super. He ordered the usual—three medium rare steaks and chopped steak for Shawn.

"I think I'll skip the steak," I said before the waitress had a chance to write the order. "I'll just have a large tossed salad."

"No steak?" my father asked, puzzled.

My mother wrinkled her brow. "Heather, are you feeling all right?"

"I'm feeling great. I'm just not in the mood for anything heavy."

"She doesn't eat meat anymore," Shawn said.

I shot him my fiercest look, the little big mouth.

"No meat?" my father asked and gave a little chuckle. "What did you do? Become a vegetarian while we were away?"

"Well, not exactly. But this last week at Aunt Gloria's, I didn't touch a bit of meat. And you know what? I've been feeling so much better. More get-up-and-go. More zip."

"She's even beginning to sound like Gloria," my father said. "I always knew she took after your side of the family."

"Tell me about your vacation," I said, to change the subject.

"It was wonderful," my mother said. "Beautiful beaches, fantastic shopping, but we really missed both of you. Next time we'll make it a family vacation."

The waitress brought our food, and I dug into my salad.

"Now tell me about yourself," my mother said. "How was your stay with Shani? Poor thing. Was it terribly hard for you to fit in with the Greenwalds?"

A slice of cucumber almost slid down my throat, and I gave a little choke. "Not at all. Actually, I sort of . . . fell right in with them. Say Mom, do you think we can do some shopping this week? I could use a few new things."

"What kinds of things did you have in mind?"

I stopped eating and put my fork in the salad bowl. "Skirts," I said. "What I need mostly are skirts."

"Skirts?" My father gave me another one of his puzzled looks.

"You already have a skirt," my mother said.

"A skirt? *One* skirt?"

"But you hardly ever wear skirts, dear."

"I know I hardly ever *wore* them, but that's all changed. I'm getting tired of the same old jeans and slacks every day. I'd like to wear a skirt once in a while. Or a dress."

My father looked up from his steak. "A dress? I haven't seen you in a dress since you were seven years old."

"Come on, Harvey," my mother said. "I think it's wonderful that she feels this way, and I think we should encourage her." Then she turned to me and said, "We can go Friday right after school. Dad and I won't be going out in the evening. I think we've had enough running around for a while."

"No, not Friday," I said. "I'll probably be busy."

"Saturday, then. We'll go shopping, have lunch . . . just like old times."

"No, not Saturday. It's not a good day for shopping."

"Since when hasn't Saturday been a good shopping day?"

"It's too crowded. Just mobs and mobs of pushers and shovers. You can't even concentrate on what you're buying. How about one evening during the week?"

"Whenever you say," my mother said.

After school on Thursday we went to Ohrbach's where I picked up a casual dress, three skirts, and a few tops—including a blue bulky knit which the saleslady said matched my eyes. Now I would be all set for Friday nights, Saturdays, holidays, whatever.

"Which outfit do you think I should wear to Shani's tomorrow?" I asked when we were driving home.

"You're going to Shani's tomorrow?"

"They invited me for dinner."

"But you've been there for a month of dinners," my mother said. "Aren't you and Shani a little tired of all that togetherness?"

"I guess we've gotten used to each other."

"All the same, I don't think we should take advantage of the Greenwalds' hospitality."

"I'm not taking advantage. I'm taking Beth's place. So it's more like doing them a favor."

"To me it still sounds like we're imposing on them."

"But what about the tablecloth? Mrs. Greenwald said she'd be using it, and I want to see how it looks."

"You'll see how it looks some other time," my mother said. "Besides, what would you eat now that you're off meat? Or are you back on it?"

"No, I'm still off," I said, a little put out that she should take my new diet so lightly. "I'll just eat the stuff around it."

"I don't want you going there for meals quite so soon," my mother said as she pulled up in front of the house. And I knew the subject was closed.

"But what will you do for *Shabbos*?" Shani asked when I called her that evening to uninvite myself.

"I don't know. I'll think of something, I guess."

"Come over after school tomorrow and I'll help you think."

The next morning I did a little thinking during home ec, and got so far as realizing that I didn't have any candles for the candleholders I brought home from Shani's house. That's as far as I got because Mrs. Rosencrans burst into the room and began passing out some papers. My eyes followed her, this *zoftig* lady with white knee socks and hairy legs. She

95

wore a green vest with a white blouse that had large red flowers on it. She looked like a walking flower bouquet.

Audrey and I managed to get stuck in home ec together. We wanted to take shop, but so did everyone else in school, and it was almost impossible to get in. Roseann made it, but Audrey and I were doomed to a year of folding napkins. It was Mrs. Rosencrans's hobby. She teaches us to fold napkins in all kinds of creative ways. In the shape of fans and flowers.

"I want everyone to pay special attention to what I've just passed out," Mrs. Rosencrans was saying. "It's never too early to think about your future."

I glanced at the sheet expecting to find instructions for another napkin folding, and wondering what that had to do with my future. I couldn't believe it! I was staring at an application to a four-year macrame college.

"Wheeee," one kid cried out from the back of the room. "I've always wanted to go to med school, but now I think I'll go to macrame college instead."

Mrs. Rosencrans became somewhat miffed. "Whoever doesn't want it just pass it up to the front," she said, and the entire class sent them back to her.

"That woman is something else," I said to Audrey on our way out of the room. We stopped off at my locker to pick up my tuna sandwich.

"You brought your lunch again?" Audrey asked. "I thought you liked what we're having today."

"What are we having?"

"I don't remember. But I know it was something you liked."

We spotted Roseann at the candy machine where she was peeling the wrapper off a Mr. Goodbar. Roseann loves peanuts.

"Right before lunch?" I asked.

"I couldn't wait," Roseann said, and began chomping away.

We walked into the cafeteria, where I lent Audrey lunch money because she forgot hers as usual, and then I got in line for a carton of chocolate milk. I found seats next to some boys from the debating team and waited for Audrey and Roseann. The boys were having a heated argument about a Three Stooges movie they saw on TV.

"It was Moe who said that."

"No, it was Larry."

"You're both wrong. It was Curly."

"For God's sake," I said under my breath.

Audrey and Roseann came over with their chili and chocolate milk. Chili was always one of my favorites. But certainly never with chocolate milk. The combination seemed especially unappetizing now.

Audrey and Roseann fought over who would sit closest to the boys. Audrey won. Roseann shrugged and wrinkled up her nose. "Maybe I'll have better luck at the bowling alley tonight." She blew into her chili bowl and began eating.

"What time should we pick you up?" she asked me after a while. "It's been so long since you've gone with us I can't even remember."

"I'm not going tonight either."

She looked up from her chili and stared at me. "Not going? How come? You don't have to stay at Shani's anymore."

"I know, but my mom and dad just came back and I don't feel like running out on them so soon."

"First you won't run out on Shani, and now you won't run out on your own mother and father. Sometimes I don't understand you, Heather."

"Let's go tomorrow night," I suggested.

"I think I'm baby-sitting," Audrey said.

"Sunday night, then."

"It's not the same," Roseann said.

Right after school I went over to Shani's house. I knew she'd be home already because she has school for just half a day on winter Fridays. I rang the bell and put my finger over the peephole so she couldn't see who it was.

"I've been waiting for you," Shani said as soon as she opened the door.

"How did you know it was me? You could've been opening up to a complete stranger."

"I could recognize your finger. Come on in."

Even before I stepped inside I was overcome by the familiar aroma of chicken soup and Saturday *cholent*. "Mmmm, it smells so good in here," I said, and inhaled.

"I'm wearing your mother's perfume."

"It's not the perfume," I said. "Shani, I need some candles for tonight. I didn't get a chance to buy any."

"No problem. Let's go into the kitchen, and I'll get you some."

"Thanks. But look, I don't want your mom to see."

"She won't. She's upstairs getting dressed. But she'd be thrilled to know that you were lighting candles on Friday night."

I caught her by the arm. "You didn't tell her about me, did you?"

"Of course not. I won't say anything if you don't want me to."

"Good. Because I still don't want anyone else to know about my conversion. Something might slip out to my mom and dad."

"Okay, whatever you say." She grabbed a batch of candles from a large box and dumped them in a bag.

I glanced around the kitchen, at the aluminum-foil packages and the pots boiling on top of the stove. "Roast chicken or brisket tonight?" I asked.

"A little of both. Oh, Heather," she pleaded, "stay with us tonight."

I shook my head. "I can't."

"What will you eat then?"

"What I've been eating all week. Tuna, egg salad, peanut butter . . ."

"Just as I thought," she said, and she went into the pantry and came out with a foot-long kosher salami.

"What in the . . ."

"Your dinner, Miss Hopkowitz. Not exactly a Sabbath dinner, but it's the best I could do under the circumstances."

"Boy, this is really something," I said. I felt like devouring the entire salami right then and there. "But I can't take it. What if your mother finds out she's minus a salami?"

"She'll never miss it."

"How can you not miss a foot-long salami?"

"She doesn't even know about it. I just bought it for you this afternoon."

"No kidding? You really did that for me?" I was very touched. Nobody ever bought me a salami before.

I stuffed the salami inside my jacket and put the bag of candles into my purse. "I'm paying you back for all this," I told Shani. "First thing Sunday."

"No you're not. Because if that's what you plan to do, I'm taking everything back."

"No chance," I said, and hugged her. "I'll see you tomorrow."

I let myself into the house and ran up to my room. Thank God I have the luxury of privacy. Still hanging from the knob of my bedroom door was the sign I had lifted from a motel in Niagara Falls. On one side of it was Do Not Disturb, in three different languages. English, French, and Spanish. And the other side, which I use more often—as a hint to my mother—said Maid, Please Make Up This Room, also in English, French, and Spanish. My mother is not impressed. She refuses to even step inside my room unless I make an effort to pick up after myself— which I don't. It was a pretty safe bet that as long as I had the "Maid" sign up, she wouldn't enter my room. But to be on the safe side, I put the candles in the drawer with my candleholders and hung up my salami in the closet. Then I ran downstairs.

My mother was on the phone, and Shawn was in the den, listening to a record and having some milk and cookies. I sat down next to him and watched him dunk vanilla wafers in a glass of milk.

"Want some?" he asked.

"Do you have any dry ones?"

"No, they're all in here," he said, and dipped his hand into the milk to retrieve a soggy cookie.

"I suddenly don't have an appetite," I said.

"Some mail came for you today," my mother announced, walking into the den.

"Mail? From who?"

"From your dad and me. 'We're drinking "yellow birds" in Montego Bay.' "

"It's not polite to read someone else's mail," I said and took the postcard from her. "What are 'yellow birds'?"

"Rum and pineapple juice. Are you coming with us for pizza tonight or are you going bowling?"

"Well, you know Audrey and Roseann, especially Roseann. They have a fit if I don't go with them. Anyway, they said something about going for pizza too."

"It's a shame you had to miss out on so much all month."

"It wasn't so bad," I said.

About twenty minutes before sunset, I went up to my room, changed into one of my new outfits, and took out two candles from the drawer and my candle-holders. I placed the candles in the holders and set them down on my dresser after I had cleared it of all its clutter. Then I lit the candles, said the blessing, and welcomed the Sabbath Queen. I should welcome her with a song, I thought, and tried humming the ones that I heard at the *Shabbaton*. It was no use. I couldn't remember anything. But it didn't matter. The room was warm and all aglow and I knew the Sabbath Queen was with me.

I sliced up some salami and nibbled on it. Not a feast, but not bad. Not bad at all. Next week there would be something better. Good food, challah, and sweet red wine. No doubt about it, next week I'd be prepared.

10

I woke up at eight the next morning, which surprised even me. I had never gotten up before ten o'clock on a Saturday, except when I was staying with Shani. My mother and I always loved sleeping late while my father went to work and Shawn watched cartoons on TV.

I went into the closet to pick out something to wear. When I opened the door I was greeted by a whiff of garlic. The whole closet smelled like a salami factory. I opened a window to let the cold air in. Then I hung up my skirt and blouse on the back of a chair so they'd air out while I washed up.

By the time I got around to putting my blouse on it felt like an ice pack. But at least some of the smell was gone. I doused myself with cologne for security.

I could hear the TV going and my mother typing in the den when I went downstairs.

"You're up early," I said from the doorway.

"I know," my mother answered without looking up from her typing. "I wanted to get an early start on 'Stowaway.' I dreamed up some pretty good ideas during the night." It always amazes me that my mother can talk and type at the same time.

"And speaking of early," she said, "what's *your* excuse?"

"I'm going jogging," I said.

My mother stopped typing, but kept her fingers on the keys and her eyes on her paper. "Jogging?" she asked, to reassure herself that she was hearing right. Then she turned her head toward me and looked me up and down.

"In a skirt?"

"All my pants are dirty."

"And high-heeled boots?"

Shawn got up from the floor where he was watching TV and came over. He walked around me and sniffed. "You smell funny," he said.

"No, I don't. You just don't appreciate quality cologne."

"Heather, come on now," my mother said. "You're not really going jogging in this snow, are you?"

"Well, no. I'm just going out for an early-morning walk."

"Alone?"

"No, I plan on going with a few friends."

104

"Is this part of your new health routine?"

"Well, sort of. But look, if you don't want me to go, it's okay. I can just go back upstairs and sleep away the morning."

"No, of course not." She waved me off.

"I'll be back in time for lunch," I said, and went over to Shani's.

"You went a little heavy on the cologne, didn't you?" Shani asked when we were walking to the synagogue.

"It's better than garlic," I said, and I told her about the salami in the closet. "Now I've got it hanging from the inside doorknob in my bedroom."

It was a little after nine by the time we reached the synagogue. Heshy and Scott walked in right after us.

"Hi, Heshy. Hi, Scott," I said.

"Call me Shimon," Scott said. "That's my new name. I'm only Scott to my mother and father."

"You finally decided on a Hebrew name?" Shani asked him.

"With a little help from my friend here," Scott-Shimon said, patting Heshy on the back.

"Well, I just helped him narrow it down a little," Heshy answered. "Shimon was his own choice. It means 'hearing, with acceptance.' "

"It's sort of like I heard the call and accepted," Scott-Shimon explained. "But mostly I just like the name."

"What do your parents think of your new name?" I asked him, and wondered what my own mother and father would say if I came home with a Hebrew name.

"Are you kidding? They don't even know about it. Eventually they'll find out, but why rush it?"

Exactly, I thought. That's how I would've handled it if I took a Hebrew name.

If I took a Hebrew name . . . the idea implanted itself in my head almost immediately, and it kept pushing its way in, deeper and deeper as the services went on, until it was firmly rooted in my mind. Of course. Why not? A new name to fit the new me. I loved it!

I nudged Shani. "I want a new name," I whispered.

"What's wrong with Heather?"

"You know what I mean. I want a Hebrew name."

"Do you have any in mind?"

"None at all. I was hoping you'd have some ideas."

"Maybe something biblical," Shani said, and she reached over to the divider, which also serves as a bookshelf, and handed me a Bible.

I began at the beginning and leafed through the pages. I skimmed through the parts about Abraham and Sarah, Isaac and Rebecca, and Jacob and his Rachel and Leah. Maybe I could be one of the matriarchs. Sarah or Rebecca, Rachel or Leah. Maybe Rebecca.

"What's the Hebrew name for Rebecca?" I asked Shani.

"Rivka," she said.

Rivka. I turned the name over and over in my mind. Rivka Hopkowitz. Rivka Hopkowitz.

"I don't know," I said to Shani. "I'm not sure about Rivka."

"Come over later and we'll look through my name book."

We all walked out together. Shani and I, Scott, Heshy, who was followed closely by Shoshana, and Donald Gluck, who was back to blinking again. I think Donald liked Shani even though she wasn't interested in his crayons anymore. He went out of his way to walk beside her.

"Are you coming to the study group this afternoon?" he asked her.

"I don't think there's going to be one," she said.

"There isn't," Shoshana said. "Kevin is still on vacation. That's the reason you didn't get any notice in the mail. And speaking of mail," she said to me, "you ought to join up, Heather. Membership is just five dollars. That means you can join the activities for less than nonmembers and receive all the bulletins and notices in the mail."

That's just what I needed. All those synagogue mailings—the way my mother hangs out at the mailbox. *"Heather, why are you suddenly getting so much mail from this synagogue?"*

"Oh, didn't I tell you? I joined an Orthodox youth group."

"I plan to," I told Shoshana. "I just haven't gotten around to doing anything yet."

107

We said good-bye to Shoshana and Donald at the next corner. A block later Heshy and I dropped off Shani and Scott.

"See you this afternoon, Shani," I said. "So long, Shimon."

He smiled at me and waved.

"He certainly likes being called Shimon," I said to Heshy.

"He sure does. But I still think of him as Scott. I guess it'll take some getting used to. Come on, Heather, I'll walk you home."

What? I screamed to myself. Walk me home? Have my mother see you wearing that *kipa*? Oh, the irony of it all. To have to turn down the first great-looking boy—or any boy for that matter—who offers to walk me home.

"You don't have to, Heshy. It's probably out of your way."

"Not very. And I'm in no hurry."

We started walking together and I almost slipped on the ice, I was so nervous. Heshy caught my arm and helped me gain my balance. That made me even more nervous. I kept looking at his bare head. It was cold out. Why wasn't he wearing a ski cap?

It began to snow and we walked together in silence. Heshy soon broke the silence.

"What's *your* Hebrew name, Heather?"

That was a good question. What was it, anyway? Rivka? Rivka Hopkowitz? I didn't feel like a Rivka.

"I don't have one," I said. "What's yours? Your full name, I mean."

"Hershel. I used to be called Hershy for short. But every once in a while some wise guy would call me a Hershey bar. So I changed Hershy to Heshy. Hardly anyone calls me a Heshy bar." He smiled at me, and I melted like a Hershey bar left out too long in the sun.

As we walked I concentrated on stepping in the snow in places where no one had walked before.

"I love making footprints in the snow," I said.

"So do I," said Heshy. "When I was a kid, I used to like to follow footprints, too. I'd pick out a pair and follow them as far as I could to see where they would lead me. I thought it was real detective work."

"Then follow these prints and see where they lead you," I said, walking up ahead. And he followed my footprints all the way to my house. Heshy's hair was all white by the time we got there. The snow covered his *kipa* and I was able to relax while we talked in front of the house for a few minutes before he left.

Shawn greeted me at the door with "Who's that boy you were talking to?"

"What boy?"

My mother came into the living room. "Yes, what boy?"

"Oh, him? Just a kid from school. I'm starved. What's to eat?"

"Let's go out to lunch," my mother said. "Then we'll go shopping or to a movie."

"A movie!" Shawn cried out.

"You two go," I said. "I'm kind of tired."

"Do you feel sick?" my mother asked, putting her

109

hand on my forehead. "You've never refused lunch and shopping before. It must be that diet of yours."

"It's not the diet," I said. "It's probably from all that walking. And look how early I woke up."

In the kitchen I made myself a cheese sandwich and poured a glass of milk. A few minutes later my mother came in, holding up a postcard.

"Another card just came for you. This one's from Nassau."

"Gee, I never realized I was so popular." She handed me the card and I read parts of it out loud.

" ' . . . We are enjoying the pristine waters, the powdery white sand beaches and star-dusted nights.' Hey, Mom, that's beautiful. You sound like a travel folder."

My mother took the card from me and read it to herself. "You know, this is very poetic. Maybe I'm wasting my talents on the confessions."

The ringing telephone snapped my mother out of her reverie.

"Oh, Heather, would you get that?"

My first Saturday phone call disturbing the quiet of the Sabbath. It's not permissible to speak on the telephone on *Shabbos*. So I wasn't going to answer it.

"Get what?" I asked.

"The phone. It's ringing. Oh, never mind. I'll get it myself."

While my mother was talking, the doorbell rang and I went to answer it. Roseann and Audrey were at the door. Roseann was wearing her furry brown coat and holding a pile of magazines.

"Do you want to come with us to the beauty parlor to watch them cut hair?" she asked. And then, as if she only just saw me, added, "Why are you all dressed up?"

"I'm going away," I said. "But come on in for a few minutes."

My mother burst in on us while they took their things off. "Hi, kids. Did you enjoy your walk this morning?"

"They always enjoy walking," I said, and shooed them into the den.

"What kind of walk was your mother talking about?" Audrey asked as she flopped down on the sofa.

"She just meant did you have a nice walk over here. What's all this about going to the beauty parlor?"

"I'm looking for a new hairstyle," Audrey said. "And I thought I might get some ideas at the beauty parlor. I can't make up my mind if I should keep it long or cut it short."

"Cut it," Roseann said. "Sometimes your hair gets so messed up you can't even see your face." She sat down next to Audrey and began poring through her pile of hairdo magazines. Then she handed each of us a magazine and ordered us to find something.

"Some of these are horrendous," Audrey said.

I leafed through my magazine but couldn't find

111

anything that looked like Audrey. Somehow I couldn't picture her with any other hairstyle.

"There's nothing here," I said. "Maybe you'll have better luck at the beauty parlor."

"Are you sure you can't come with us?" Audrey asked.

I can't, Audrey. While you go looking for a new hairstyle, I'll be out looking for a new name.

"I'm going away," I said.

"You've been making yourself awfully scarce lately," Audrey said as we walked to the door.

"Not on purpose, though. Lots of things have been coming up."

"Well, I hope everything gets back to normal soon."

"I hope so too," I said, knowing full well that nothing would get back to normal ever again.

Fifteen minutes later I was knocking on the Greenwald door.

Mrs. Greenwald answered. "You're just in time," she said.

"I am?"

"Shani's on her second lunch. And I still have a whole pot of *cholent* simmering on the stove."

Cholent? Let me at it! I took off my coat and boots.

"I missed being here last night," I said. "At least I won't have to miss your *cholent*."

"Well, we missed having you here, Heather." Then she put her arm around me and brought me into the kitchen.

"Perfect timing," Shani said, looking up from her

plate. "Let me get you some." She started to get up from her chair, but I stopped her.

"Don't bother. I know where everything is, remember?"

I lifted the lid off the pot and a light steam came out to meet me. I breathed in deeply, savoring the aroma, and then I dipped the spoon in and brought out the meat and barley, beans, and potatoes. Oh, how can a cheese sandwich compare to this?

I took my plate back to the table and sat down across from Shani. "This reminds me of the olden days," I said. "Way back when my grandmother brought me here and we all ate lunch at your kitchen table. Remember?"

"We had fun together, that's for sure," Shani said. "But to tell you the truth, some of my memories are a little fuzzy."

"Mine were too, for a long time. But lately so much has come back to me. It's sort of like I'm getting in touch with myself."

Mr. Greenwald popped in to say hello and then both he and Mrs. Greenwald popped out to go visiting, leaving Shani and me alone in the kitchen over our *cholent* and Shani's Hebrew name book.

"How about Ahava?" Shani said, picking a name from the *A* column. "It means 'love.' Or Aviva, 'spring'?"

"I don't know," I said. "What do you have in the way of *B*'s?" *B* was one of my favorite letters.

"Okay, let's see. There's Batya, 'daughter of God.' Or Batsheva, as in David and Bathsheba."

"Hmmm, Batsheva. Batsheva Hopkowitz. Oh, I don't know. I'm not sure about that either."

"Look," she said, closing her name book. "You don't have to make up your mind right now. Take Batsheva home with you and try it on. Wear it for a while and see if it fits. If you don't like it, bring it back and we'll get you something else." She sounded like a shoe salesperson.

So Batsheva and I went home, and after sundown, when the Sabbath was over, I went up to my room and practiced writing Batsheva Hopkowitz in my notebook. Seeing it written down would make it easier to believe.

There was a knock on the door and I stopped writing.

"Who is it?"

"It's me," said Shawn.

"What do you want?"

"Come down to eat. Daddy brought some stuff home from the fish place."

Oh boy, lox and smoked whitefish, I'll bet.

"I'll be right there," I said, and slipped my notebook into the desk drawer.

Shawn and I skipped down the stairs together, and when we got to the kitchen I stopped in my tracks. I stared at the table in disbelief. My lox and smoked whitefish had turned into shrimp, lobster, and clam dip. All of it one hundred percent non-kosher.

"Some spread, huh?" my father said when he saw me with my mouth open. "All your favorites. Kind of caught you by surprise, didn't it?"

"Sure did," I said, still staring. Where's my lox?

"Well, don't just stand there. Sit down and eat something."

"I can't," I said. "I can't eat that."

"Why can't you eat that?" my mother asked when she brought some plates to the table.

"Because that's seafood. And I can't. I'm . . . abstaining. I'm abstaining from all living creatures."

"Oh, Heather, come on now," my mother said, throwing some napkins on the table in disgust. "I thought you'd be off that kick by now. I just wish you would start eating like a normal person again."

"Those are animals over there," I said. "And it's not right to eat them. It's inhuman." It's funny how I was almost beginning to believe myself. Still, I didn't feel right about the lying.

"You know, Heather," my father said, filling up his plate, "I don't like the way you look."

"Well, thanks a lot," I said, and I sat down and nibbled on a slice of cucumber.

"You're looking pale and thin—which comes from not eating right. And if you keep giving everything up, there won't be anything left for you to eat. You'll dry up and wither away."

My father was right. Pretty soon there wouldn't be anything left. Me and my big mouth. I'm abstaining from all living creatures. Ha. Why couldn't I have just said I wasn't hungry? Why did I have to give up the little I had left? Well, too late. Good-bye tuna, good-bye salmon, good-bye lox and smoked whitefish.

The next morning we all went to see Grandpa. Even my mother, who decided it was about time for her to visit. Grandpa was sitting in his chair, sleeping, when we got there, so my mother and father took Shawn for a walk around the building. I wanted to wait in Grandpa's room, so I sat down in a chair across the room from him and watched him sleep.

How white his hair was. And his skin. So smooth and clear. I hoped mine would be that way at his age. First though, I'd have to get rid of my acne.

His glasses and book were on a table next to him, and I went over to see what he'd been reading. It was a book of Jewish folklore. Grandpa loved those stories, and when I was small, I used to enjoy sitting on his lap and listening to a story he was reading to me. I remember one that was always my favorite. I remember now that I liked it even more than "The Three Bears" or "Little Red Riding Hood." It was about a man who complained to the rabbi that his house was too small and overcrowded.

"Do as I tell you," said the rabbi. "Bring your cow into your house. And your goat, and your chickens too."

So the man did as he was told. But now things were even worse. So he went back to the rabbi and said, "Rabbi, my house is like a barn. And there's so much noise. It's worse than ever."

"Take out the cow," said the rabbi. "And your goat, and your chickens."

Again the man did as he was told. And the next

day he went back to the rabbi and said, "Oh, Rabbi, everything is quiet and peaceful now. And there's so much room! How can I ever thank you?"

Just thinking about the story made me laugh out loud. Maybe that's what woke Grandpa.

"Caught me napping, eh?"

"It looks that way," I said, and went over and kissed him on the forehead. "The others will be here in a little while."

I sat down on the edge of the bed. "Say, Grandpa, what do you think of the name Batsheva?"

"It's a nice name," he said. "Who's Batsheva?"

"I'm not sure yet, but it might be me."

He raised his eyebrows, and I could see a huge question mark on his face.

"I've got some news I want to tell you, Grandpa," I said, "and Batsheva is part of it." I glanced at the door to make sure nobody was there and then I went on.

"Remember how I was telling you that I was going to *shul* on Saturdays? Well, I'm still going. And I've started to light my own candles on Friday nights, and I'm trying to keep kosher, and I'm looking for a Hebrew name."

"And you're thinking of Batsheva."

"Maybe Batsheva, but maybe something else."

He nodded and smiled—more to himself than to me.

"Well . . . what can I say to all this? . . . I think it's wonderful news." And then as an afterthought, he

117

asked, "What do your mother and father say?"

"Nothing. They don't know anything about it. I've managed to keep it quiet so far."

"Don't you think you owe it to them to let them know how you feel?"

"I'd like to be able to, Grandpa, but it wouldn't serve any purpose—except to get them all upset. Especially my mother. You know how she'd feel."

I got up and walked over to him. "Grandpa, do you think it's wrong, what I'm doing? Being observant when I know they'd be so against it? Am I cheating them?"

"If you're acting from your heart, if you're acting out of a true belief, then any other way you would be cheating yourself. And who knows? Maybe in time you'll be able to tell them, and they'll accept it."

"I sure hope it turns out that way, Grandpa. But I seriously doubt it."

"Bend down a little," Grandpa said, "and look right into my eyes."

I did as he asked, half expecting him to work a bit of his magic by plucking a piece of candy from behind my ear. He looked straight at me and smiled. "You know," he said, "today you remind me very much of your grandmother."

The phone was ringing when we walked into the house after visiting Grandpa. My mother went to answer it.

"You must have the wrong number," she said, and

118

hung up. "Some girl called for Batsheva," she told us.

"Did you tell her she was with David?" I asked, and ran upstairs to call Shani.

"Oh, Heather, I'm so sorry, I could die," Shani said as soon as she heard my voice. "But I thought I was talking to you, so I said, 'Hi, Batsheva.' Honestly, sometimes you and your mother sound exactly alike on the phone. I hope I didn't give away the secret."

It was kind of funny in a way. When I heard my mother say the name, I knew that Batsheva wasn't me either.

"Don't worry, Shani. You didn't give away any secrets. You see, Batsheva doesn't live here anymore."

11

During the next week my mother borrowed a meat-less cookbook from Aunt Gloria and I borrowed Shani's name book. And while my mother whipped up mock hamburger made from soybeans, I chose and discarded name after name.

Zipporah ("bird").

Ilana ("tree").

On Wednesday I became Ora ("light"). I called Shani to tell her.

"You can call me Ora," I said.

"For how long?"

"I don't know. I might keep this one. Ora Hop-kowitz. Because I've seen the light. It's meaningful. Will you come with me to buy some things for *Shabbos*?"

"Sure. Come over after school tomorrow and we'll get whatever you need."

I walked home with Audrey and Roseann the next day.

"I still think you're crazy," Roseann was saying to Audrey. "I never heard of anyone asking to get a grade lowered."

They were talking about Audrey's midterm grade in home ec. Mrs. Rosencrans gave both of us A−. And Audrey asked to have hers changed to a B+.

"Why did you do such a thing?"

"I'd rather get a strong B than a weak A," Audrey said. "And Mrs. Rosencrans agreed with me. She also thinks I should let my hair grow long."

"You mean to tell me you consulted Mrs. Rosencrans about your hair?" I asked. "You actually sought the advice of a teacher who has hairy legs, wears white knee socks, and once yelled at you for being lefthanded? Well, all I can say is if she told you to grow it long, then by all means cut it."

"Hey," Roseann said, "why don't we stop somewhere and look at some new magazines for ideas?"

"I can't," I said. "I've got to go shopping."

"For what?"

"Oh, just lots of little things."

"And what about tomorrow?"

"I'm sitting for Shawn."

"It figures," Roseann said.

I dropped my books off at the house, took my life savings out of my sneaker bank, and went over to Shani's.

"What do you want to buy first?" she asked when we started out.

"I'll need some challah," I said, "and some grape juice."

I had decided on grape juice instead of wine. Somehow it didn't seem right for a fourteen-year-old girl to be hiding up in her room drinking wine. Even for sacramental purposes.

With Shani as a guide, I bought two small loaves of challah at a kosher bakery, a small bottle of grape juice at a kosher deli, a barbecued chicken breast at a kosher carry-out, and for starters, two plastic plates (one for meat and one for dairy) and some silverware at Woolworth's. (Although the initial investment for this was substantial, in the long run it would be cheaper than paper plates and plastic forks.) Eventually I would buy some cooking utensils and a hot plate.

"That should do it," Shani said. "Unless you can think of something else."

"I don't think there's anything. Anyway, I'm all out of money."

Shani and I parted at the corner and then I walked home with my shopping bag. Now—how to get all the stuff into the house with nobody knowing. I left my bag outside and went in to case the place. My mother was straightening up the den to make it look like she spent all day cleaning instead of all day writing, and Shawn was there with her, spraying Endust on the furniture.

All clear. I ran back out for my bag, and then upstairs to put everything away. On a shelf went my dishes, silverware, and challah in its plastic bag. I sneaked down to the basement to retrieve our Igloo ice chest, which I washed out and brought back up to my room.

I filled up two bowls with some ice from our refrigerator, which has an automatic ice cube maker, and dumped the ice into the Igloo. There was more than enough to keep my grape juice chilled and my chicken from spoiling. All finished. I was so proud of myself.

"Hey, Heather!"

"What?" I spun around. "Shawn, what are you doing here? I hope you know that you enter this room without permission only under penalty of death."

"The door was open—sort of. So I just walked in."

"Well, now you can just walk out."

"What's all that food for?"

I put my arm around him. "Listen, Shawn, this food is for charity."

"Who's she?"

"Charity is something you give to the poor. I'm giving this food to a person who's very hungry. But you mustn't tell anyone about it."

"Why not?"

"Because charity is very personal and private. No one is supposed to know who's giving it and who's getting it. Do you understand?"

He shook his head.

"Well, it doesn't matter. Just promise you won't

say anything to anybody. This will be our secret. Promise?"

"Promise."

"Okay, now why don't you go downstairs, and I'll be down in a few minutes." After he left, I checked to make sure everything was in its place. Then I walked out and shut the door behind me, leaving the Maid, Please Make Up This Room sign hanging from the knob.

Shani had given me a chart listing the candle lighting times for the entire year, so I knew just when to light the candles that Friday evening. I lit the candles; wished myself a Good *Shabbos*—"Good *Shabbos*, Ora"; poured myself a small glass of grape juice—small so the juice would last a long time; and cut myself a piece of challah. And over everything I said the proper blessings. I said them in English because I didn't know the Hebrew words yet. I'd learn them one day, I promised myself. Blessings are more authentic when they're in Hebrew.

I finished off the chicken in five bites. It was a small breast. Then I went downstairs with my excuse for not going out with Audrey and Roseann. "I'm getting awfully sick of doing the same thing week after week," I said.

"If you're not going out, why are you all dressed up?" my mother asked. I was wearing my Sabbath clothes.

"I didn't want you to think you wasted your money on all the stuff you bought me, so I'm putting everything to good use."

124

At dinnertime I made an appearance at the table for a salad, and then I spent the evening reading to Shawn from *Winnie-the-Pooh* and dodging telephone calls. I made it my business to run to the bathroom every time I heard the phone ring.

I went to *shul* on Saturday and said I was going to the beauty parlor to watch them cut hair, and then I came home to dodge more phone calls.

"If it's for me I'm not home."

"Why aren't you home?" my mother asked.

"It's probably Audrey or Roseann and I'm not in the mood to sit around engaging in idle conversation."

I also declined an invitation to ride out to see Aunt Gloria. "I'm not in the mood for a long drive today," I told my mother.

"You're not in the mood for lots of things lately," she said, helping Shawn put on his fur-lined cowboy boots. "And it's not a long ride. She lives just fifteen minutes away."

"I get carsick."

"Since when?"

"Since lots of times. I just never mentioned it before."

The next week when I went to the synagogue I said I was invited to Audrey's for breakfast. And to make sure Audrey wouldn't spoil things by calling or coming over, I had to tell her I was going to Shani's for breakfast. It's frightening to realize how easy it is to get into the habit of lying.

The biggest problem I had was with the food. I

had long since finished off my salami and I had run out of money to buy anything else. My ice chest was an empty, sorry sight. I had many times dumped the water out of it and replenished it with enough ice to keep my grape juice cold. But I was hungry. It wasn't that my mother didn't try hard to feed me. She really did. But meatless meals weren't her specialty. And they weren't mine either. Though she did a fair job of frying eggplant and she did make some pretty good stuffed peppers. I even complimented her on her efforts.

"I hope you know that I really appreciate your making all these special meals for me," I said.

"Well, why not? The food is nourishing and much tastier than I ever imagined it would be. And if this is what it takes to keep you going, then I'm all for it. I'm certainly not about to let you go hungry."

But I *was* hungry. For meat! I needed meat, meat, meat! Stop it, Ora, I told myself. You're not a cannibal. You're not carnivorous. You don't need the flesh of animals for survival, do you?

Oh, yes. Yes I do.

We had just come back from visiting Grandpa one Sunday, where I had informed him of my new name. Shira ("song"). Shira Hopkowitz. It had a nice ring. I had first considered the name Shifra ("beautiful") but I discarded it. I was not beautiful. And besides, Shani's name means "beautiful" too, and I didn't want her to think I was competing.

Grandpa laughed when he heard that I changed

my name again—and again. "Oh, if only your Grandma could see you now. She would be so proud of you. You were always very special to her, you know." And it was this thought of being special that I took home with me that day.

Well, anyway, we had just come home, and my father went back out to pick up some goodies for dinner. I expected shrimp and he came back with corned beef. I could smell it the minute he walked into the house. Hot corned beef. I could feel the heat right through the bag. I could see the lean beef reveal itself as he unwrapped it from the white paper from Farfel's kosher delicatessen. FILL YOUR BELI AT FARFEL'S DELI. What was that? A kosher delicatessen? The corned beef was kosher? Hallelujah! Kosher corned beef. I could eat at last. See, Shira, good things come to those who wait. Then someone stuck a pin in me and let out all the air. I couldn't eat it. It was kosher and I COULD NOT EAT IT! I was a vegetarian.

"This is kosher," I informed my father.

"What's so surprising? I've bought kosher corned beef before."

I was furious. Of all the nerve. How dare they? How dare they bring kosher corned beef into this house?

I turned and started up the stairs.

"Your eggplant is ready," came my mother's voice after me.

"I'm not hungry," I said. I turned my sign around to Do Not Disturb and shut the door.

127

"Shani? It's me. Shira."

"Shira?"

"You know. Heather."

"Oh, hi Heather. I mean Shira. You don't sound like yourself."

"Oh, Shani. I'm so hungry. I need some real food."

"Heather, please let me tell my mother about you. She'd be happy to fix up a CARE package for you."

"You can't do that," I told her. "You'd be involving her in a conspiracy. She'd be torn between loyalty to me and an obligation to tell my mother. She'd feel guilty, she'd . . ."

"Okay, okay, I get the point. But at least come to dinner Friday. You can get away, can't you?"

"I'll get away, all right. I don't know how yet, but I will."

I suddenly felt the need to go bowling again.

"I thought you were sick of bowling," my mother said that Friday morning.

"I've recovered," I said.

I told Audrey and Roseann I was busy again. Although I didn't bother to give any specific excuses. It was too exhausting to think of any more excuses. And lest they were beginning to think I was avoiding them, I made my usual suggestion. "Why can't we go on Sunday when it's easier for me to get away? Either before or after I go to see my grandfather."

"Then we wouldn't be celebrating TGIF," Roseann said.

Audrey was puzzled. "TGIF?"

"Thank God It's Friday," Roseann explained.

In addition to satisfying my cannibal instincts at dinner that night, I also made a discovery. I discovered that I knew Hebrew. Six words of Hebrew.

The table was all set when I arrived at Shani's house. And on the table a third pair of candleholders was waiting for me.

"I thought you might like to light some candles with us," Shani said in a way that wouldn't make her mother suspicious.

"Okay," I said. "I'll give it a try."

After we lit the candles, Shani's mother said the blessing to herself. But Shani said it loud enough for me to follow. The thing is, I didn't need to follow—in the beginning. I found that I knew the words. I counted them later and there were six of them. Those same words that began the blessing over the candles also began the blessing over the challah. They were part of the *kiddush* over the wine. Just six words. But it was a beginning.

I tried not to appear too hungry, but I devoured the chopped liver, the rib roast, and two bowls of chicken soup with matzo balls. We ate and sang, and · it was as if I hadn't missed even a single Friday night in their home.

On Saturday I said I was going ice-skating at the arena so I could go to the synagogue.

"You'll need some money," my mother said.

"I have some," I said.

"Enough for admission and skate rental?"

"Oh, sure," I said, feeling rotten again about the lying.

The services had become very familiar by now, and I didn't feel as much a stranger there anymore.

After the services there was a *kiddush* to celebrate the birth of someone's twins, and I filled up on cake and herring so I wouldn't have to worry about lunch.

"Want your onions?" Heshy asked.

He didn't have to ask. I had already set aside a pile of them for him on my plate.

"Why don't they make jars of onions with little bits of herring instead of the other way around?" he asked as he wiped the onions off my plate onto his.

"Maybe nobody ever suggested it before," I said.

Scott-Shimon walked past us and Heshy asked me, "How do you like Shimmy's *kipa*?"

"Shimmy? Oh, Shimon. It's nice. Is it new?"

"He's got his Hebrew name on this one."

"Oh, yeah. I didn't notice." I have a new name too, Heshy. Shall I tell it to you? But saying the name—Shira—would make it real. And I didn't know if I was ready for it to be real.

"Hey, Shimmy," Heshy called, and Scott-Shimon-Shimmy came over to us. "Who made it for you?" Heshy pointed to his own *kipa*.

"Sunny Margolis. A present for me in honor of my new name. I guess it's kind of a hobby for her."

Sunny Margolis. Oh, yes. The girl who didn't belong on a Dr Pepper commercial.

"How come you don't have one with your name on it?" I asked Heshy when Shimmy left.

"No one ever offered to make me one," he said.

"I'll do it," I blurted out. I tried to regain a little

130

composure. "I mean, if you'd like me to. I've had a lot of experience with pot holders." I couldn't believe how dumb I was sounding.

"Well, sure," he said. "Thanks. As long as it doesn't look like a pot holder when you're finished."

"It won't," I assured him. "What colors would you like?"

"You decide."

"And do you want your name in Hebrew or English?" I asked, hoping he'd say English.

"Hebrew."

"Oh."

"What's wrong?"

"Oh, nothing. I was just trying to think of a nice color scheme."

"Come on," Heshy said. "I'll walk you home and help you think."

I could visualize my mother at the window watching for the mailman to bring her news of "Stowaway." Oh, Heshy, you can't come home with me. It's not snowing. There'll be nothing to cover up your Jewish head.

"I wish you could, Heshy, but I'm waiting for Shani and then I'll be going over to her house."

How ironic. A small piece of cloth was keeping us apart, and I was making him yet another one. I stabbed the last piece of herring with my fork, and when I looked up from my plate, Heshy was gone. I should have offered to knit him a ski cap, I thought as I watched him walk out the door with Shoshana Katz.

12

Rain kept me from going out to buy the yarn during my free period on Monday, and nothing would have kept me from going during lunch except my shadows, Audrey and Roseann, and my empty pit of a stomach. I had brought a cheese sandwich to school but ate it during first period. So hunger sent me over to The Hangout with Audrey and Roseann, who weren't too enthusiastic about the meat loaf being served in the cafeteria.

Audrey and Roseann ordered hamburgers and chocolate shakes, and I asked the waitress for a tossed salad.

"That's not on the menu," she said, her pencil poised in midair.

"Can't I have it anyway?"

"I don't know. Nobody's ever ordered it before."

"If you bring me some lettuce and tomatoes I'll fix one up myself," I said.

She shook her head. "Unh uh. I don't think so. But I'll check in back and see if they'll make one for you."

"Thanks," I said. "And I'd like some salad dressing with it."

"I'll have to check on that too," she said, writing down my order.

"If you don't have any, you can bring me some ketchup and mayonnaise and I'll . . ."

"I know, I know," she interrupted. "You'll make some up yourself."

"You're not still on that diet, are you?" Roseann asked.

"Sort of," I said. "I've gotten away from meats lately."

"That's not all you've gotten away from lately," she said.

"What's that supposed to mean?"

"It means you're never around anymore."

"Sure I'm around."

"Not like before. Except for school, we never get to see you. What's going on, anyway?"

"Nothing's going on. I've just been a little busier than usual." Then to change the subject, I said, "Hey, Audrey, what have you decided about your hair?"

"Nothing yet. Right now I'm concentrating on getting contact lenses. But I can't decide if I want soft or hard."

"Get hard," Roseann suggested. "They're more durable."

"But soft are more comfortable," Audrey said.

"I hope you have better luck with yours than Donald Gluck had with his," I said.

"Who's Donald Gluck?" Audrey asked.

"Just a boy Shani knows. He either blinks all the time or gets his lenses stuck up his eyelids."

The waitress returned with the hamburgers, shakes, and salad. The salad didn't look half bad. On my plate was a small paper cup containing some orange stuff which I assumed was the dressing.

"I don't suppose you'd have any crackers around here," I said to the waitress. It was too much to hope for rolls or breadsticks.

"Of course we do," she said, acting as if she was personally insulted.

Maybe there was hope for this place after all.

"But they're only served with soup or chili."

After school Audrey and Roseann dropped me off at my corner. I circled the block and then, with my unspent bowling money, set out to buy some yarn and a jar of gefilte fish.

I had decided that a nice color scheme would be navy, red, white, and green. A navy *kipa* with a white-lettered Heshy linking a border of delicate red and white flowers with green leaves. The gefilte fish

134

was Mrs. Adler's. Twelve pieces of her special sweet recipe.

While I was in the deli, which was more like a miniature supermarket, I looked over the frozen food section and eyed the shelves. There were canned soups and frozen soups. Chicken soup with rice, noodles, matzo balls, *kreplach*; mushroom and barley and lentil. There was canned and frozen beef stew, ravioli, and chicken chow mein. And everything was kosher. The varieties seemed endless. With a pot and a hot plate (and a can opener), my possibilities would be endless.

I headed home with my yarn and special sweet recipe and approached the house with caution. I could explain away the yarn, but what could I say about my gefilte fish? I silently turned the key in the lock, opened it a crack, and listened. I could hear the TV going and the typewriter clicking, so I ran upstairs and slipped into my room.

I put the yarn away in the drawer next to the candles and opened the Igloo. My bottle of grape juice was floating around in the water, which wasn't even cold anymore, and I put in the jar of gefilte fish so they could float around together. Then I went downstairs and into the den.

"Hi," I said to my mother who was typing away like mad, totally oblivious to Shawn and the TV. If nothing else, her writing experience has turned her into a fantastic typist.

"Oh, hi honey," she said, pulling the sheet of paper out of the typewriter and waving it at me. "Page two of my new story, 'Asparagus Tore Us Apart.' " She rolled another sheet in and typed a number three at the top of the page.

"Any news about 'Stowaway'?" I asked.

She pressed a button and turned the electricity off. "Not a word. And the waiting is driving me crazy."

"Maybe they're considering it."

"And maybe it's at the bottom of a pile three feet high."

"What's this new one about?" I asked to get her back into the excitement of her latest confession.

"I'm not even sure yet. But I'm developing some very intriguing characters."

"Mom, do we happen to have an old hot plate around?"

"Why would you want a hot plate?"

"For a science experiment."

"Oh," she said in a way that indicated she didn't quite understand. "I'm afraid we don't." She turned the typewriter on again and went back to her intriguing characters.

The doorbell rang, and Shawn ran to answer it. I heard Shani's voice and ran after him. Shani had promised to get me a pattern for Heshy's *kipa*. But I never expected it so soon.

"Hi," I said when I saw her at the door doing a little warm-up dance. The cold made her cheeks look like she was wearing too much blusher.

"Hi. I can't stay long. I just came over to give you this."

She handed me a manila envelope. It was the same kind of envelope my mother uses to send out—and receive—her rejected manuscripts.

"What is it?" Shawn asked.

"Just some stuff for a pot holder," I told him. "Go back and watch your program."

"I borrowed the pattern from Sunny," Shani said. "And an instruction sheet. She said if you have a basic knowledge of crocheting, it shouldn't be too hard for you."

I opened the envelope and looked inside. The design was printed on a sheet of graph paper and a Hebrew Heshy was already penciled in for me. I even recognized two letters from the *dreidel* we used on Chanukah. The *hay* and the *shin*.

"Thanks, Shani. This is great. I'll get started right away. As soon as I figure out where I put my crochet hook."

"If you need any help, just tell me and I'll tell Sunny." She turned to leave and I stopped her.

"Shani," I said. "Do you happen to know anyone who has a hot plate?"

"Sure. Beth does. She got it for college. Lots of the kids did a little cooking up in their rooms once in a while. I'll check around and see if she left it when she went to Israel."

A few minutes after Shani left, my father came home all knocked out from an exceptionally tedious root canal job.

"A real toughie," he said at the dinner table.

"What—the steak?" my mother asked.

"No. That root canal. Had a hard time killing the nerve." He sprinkled some A-1 on his steak and cut into it. I watched him jab a piece with his fork and bring it to his mouth. I followed it all the way inside and mentally ate it with him. I would've put less A-1 on it.

My mother brought my cheese-mushroom-green pepper-tomato-onion omelet to the table. And though it looked and tasted pretty good, it wasn't steak.

"Heather, is that all you're eating?" my father asked.

"It happens to be very nourishing," my mother said.

"It's a lot healthier than steak," I added. "Did you know that Americans eat far too much meat—which accounts for the high incidence of heart trouble in this country?"

"You're right, you know," my father said, cutting another piece of steak. "But I guess I just don't have your willpower."

Willpower. Ha. I finished my omelet and went up to call Shani.

"Shani?" I said in my weak voice.

"Heather?"

"Malkah." (Malkah means "queen," and I thought it might be nice to feel queenly.)

"Okay . . . Malkah. You sound like you need another dinner."

"Oh, I'll be okay. Did you find the hot plate?"

"Not yet. I'm still looking. Did you start your pot holder?"

"I'm going to do that now. Try to take my mind off steak."

I rummaged through my drawers until I found my crochet hook. I read the beginning of the instructions and with my navy yarn started the middle circle of Heshy's *kipa*. (A little love went into each stitch, Heshy dear.)

I had a nice little circle going when the phone rang about an hour later. I picked up the receiver and said hello. Shani's voice came back at me.

"Hi, Malkah. I found it."

At the same time Shani was saying "Hi, Malkah," there was a click on the downstairs phone and my mother was saying, "Who *is* this?"

"Sorry, wrong number," Shani said quickly, and hung up.

"Mom, you still there?" I asked.

"Yes. Now that's really strange. First we get a call for Batsheva and now someone wants Malkah. What have you been doing up there for so long?"

"Homework."

"Since when do you do homework alone in your room instead of in front of the TV?"

"I find that I can no longer concentrate on homework and TV at the same time. But I'm almost finished and I'll be down in a minute."

After we both hung up I waited about ten seconds and dialed Shani's number.

"I guess I did it again, huh?" she said.

"A little close," I told her. "But no harm done. You found the hot plate?"

"Yeah. Right in my closet. And it's a real nice one. It's got an on-off switch and three temperature settings. Do you want me to bring it over tomorrow?"

"I'll pick it up. I've got to go out for food anyway."

Food was a can of kosher beef ravioli. It was all I could afford after buying my pot and can opener at Woolworth's. I then went over to Shani's to pick up the hot plate, and headed home. The house was deserted. Good. I'd make my ravioli right now. An early dinner. I could always top it off with a salad later on. With my supplies in hand, I went upstairs to set up the rest of my kitchen. My kosher kitchen.

There was an electrical outlet next to where I kept my dishes, silverware, and Igloo. I moved my old toy chest (which now served as a general junk depository) over to the wall and placed my hot plate on top of it. The chest made an excellent counter top. Oh, Malkah, you're a genius.

And now for dinner. I pierced the can with the can opener, and the tomato sauce oozed out. I emptied the contents of the can into the pot, which I had washed out, and set the hot plate on High. The tomato sauce began bubbling, slowly at first and then more rapidly. I positioned my face over the pot so as not to miss even one breath of that delicate aroma. Oh, you plump little meat pies—meat, meat, meat— all hot and bubbly, you smell so good. The smell!

In all my meticulous planning, I had forgotten

140

about the smell. It filled the whole room. Probably the whole house. I switched off the hot plate and ran to the window to let in the freezing air. With a notebook I tried to fan the aroma out the window. Out, smell, out. Next I took a can of Lysol from the linen closet and sprayed. I sprayed everywhere. My room, the upstairs hallway, and the stairwell. Then I ran downstairs to sniff. There was a curious blend of ravioli and Lysol. Oh, dear God, please don't let them come home just yet. *Heather, there seems to be a curious blend of ravioli and Lysol in the air.*

I heard the car pull up in the driveway, and I frantically began waving and blowing at the air. A key turned in the lock, the door opened, and . . .

"What stinks in here?" asked Shawn.

"What *is* that smell?" my mother asked, twitching her nose and taking off her coat.

"Lysol," I said. "Just Lysol."

"Why Lysol?"

"I'm cleaning up my room. Cleaning and airing it out."

"Now that I've got to see," my mother said, and started up the stairs.

"No, don't!" I called after her. I ran up to stop her. "Not yet. It's a mess."

"You said you cleaned it."

"I said I'm cleaning it. But you know how it is. Sometimes you have to mess up a place before you can get it to look nice. It's in worse shape than ever now. You'll hate it."

She shrugged and started back down the stairs.

"All right. In that case I'd better get that casserole in the oven."

"Maybe you can use Heather's new pot holder," Shawn suggested.

I gave him the evil eye. "I'm not finished yet," I said.

"What pot holder?" my mother asked.

"Just a pot holder I'm working on."

"Another pot holder? We've got so many of them."

"I know. But I want to keep in practice."

I went back to my room, which by now felt like Antarctica, and shut the window. Then I ate my ravioli dinner, which was preceded by a piece of gefilte fish as an appetizer. I really should have bought some horseradish to go with it.

I cleaned up the dishes and brought Heshy's *kipa* down into the den to work on while I watched TV. There was no need to stay in hiding while the *kipa* could still pass for a pot holder.

While I was crocheting and thinking of Heshy, Shawn came over to watch me. "How come this one's round?" he asked loudly enough for my mother and father to hear.

"Go to bed or something," I told him. "You're giving me a pain." Or was it just the ravioli and gefilte fish giving me heartburn?

13

Two weeks after the first loving stitch, I was standing in front of the mirror admiring Heshy's wet *kipa*. Actually, I was wearing it. The instructions said to wash the *kipa* when finished, and shape it over a bowl or your head. I chose my head. There was something intimate in the wearing.

Those two weeks of almost steady crocheting had really paid off. The *kipa* was beautiful. "Yes, D'vorah," I said to my reflection (the name means "bee," but D'vorah was also a prophetess), "this is truly a work of art."

I sent Sunny Margolis a thank-you note for her efforts, and concentrated *my* efforts on figuring out exactly when, where, and how I would present Heshy with his gift.

I thought of us together, running (in slow motion) through the fields, the March wind blowing, or sipping cocoa in a darkened cafe, or perhaps strolling under a moonlit sky, hand in hand.

But alas, the only place I ever saw Heshy was at the synagogue on Saturday mornings, and it isn't permissible to carry on the Sabbath.

An answer of sorts came one Saturday night at the end of March when Kevin Cornfield invited a bunch of us to spend an evening at his house.

Shani and I were among the last to arrive. Most of the kids were already there, standing around the table helping themselves to refreshments. Hebrew music was playing softly in the background.

My eyes searched the room for Heshy and spotted him off in a corner popping nuts or something into his mouth.

"Excuse me, Shani," I said as I hung up my coat, "but I've got to seize the moment."

"Go to it, D'vorah," she said.

The *moment* wasn't quite what I had hoped for, but it was all I had. "Aren't you afraid you'll choke doing that?" I asked Heshy just as he threw a peanut up in the air.

My unexpected greeting caused him to miss.

"Oops, sorry," I said.

"That's okay," he said, stooping to pick up the nut. "I was getting sick of them anyway." He picked up the bowl of nuts and held it out to me. "Want some?"

"No thanks, Heshy. But I have something I hope you'll want."

I reached into my purse and took out the *kipa,* appropriately wrapped in the Israeli colors, blue and white.

"What is it?" he asked.

"Go ahead and open it," I said.

I watched him tear apart the paper and waited for the second *moment.* Upon seeing his gift, Heshy would choke back tears of gratitude. His eyes would meet mine and he would say . . .

"Hey, you guys, look at this. Isn't it a beauty?"

So much for moments.

He pulled off his old *kipa,* stuffed it in his shirt pocket, and put on the new one.

"You went and made it," he said to me. "You really made it."

And I'll make you a dozen more just like it, I wanted to tell him, but I couldn't have told him even if I'd dared. Shoshana Katz had pushed her way between us and was saying, "Oh, Heshy, I would have made you one ages ago if I had known that's what you wanted."

I suppressed an urge to dump the rest of the peanuts on her head, and poured myself a Coke. I also helped myself to some shoestring potatoes, which tasted oddly like dried apples. Was I eating shoestring apples? I was mulling over this question when I heard someone ask, "Are you going next Sunday?"

I looked up. Heshy was back again, minus Shoshana, and strangely enough I no longer cared whether I was nibbling on apples or potatoes. He sat down next to me on the couch.

"What's next Sunday?" I asked.

"The concert. That's what Kevin's talking about."

I turned an ear toward the center of the room and heard Kevin saying, "If anybody needs a ride, let me know. I can squeeze about ten in my wagon."

"This is the first I've heard of it," I said.

"Well, it's no big thing, but it's a lot of fun. A small group of musicians and singers. Hebrew music, some dancing. They had it at the high school last year and it was really nice."

"In that case, maybe I'll go."

"Great. I'll pick you up."

Good God, not again. "You don't have to, Heshy. It's out of your way. Why don't I just meet you there?"

"Sure. Whatever you say." He got up and walked away.

Don't go, Heshy. You don't understand. It's not what you think.

I was desperate to talk to someone. There was Shani. But she was busy with Donald. I got up to get another handful of those shoestring things and went back to the couch with them.

"They don't taste all that bad, do they?"

"What? Oh, hi Shimmy," I said. "They're dried apples. Definitely. I couldn't make up my mind about them."

He sat down next to me in the same spot where Heshy had been sitting just a few minutes before. The spot where he'd be right now if only I weren't so cowardly.

"You did a nice job on that *kipa*," he said.

"Thanks. It was my first attempt. Sunny did a nice job on yours too."

"Yeah. But there's one big difference. Heshy can go home and show his around. He doesn't have to keep it a big secret. I had mine for almost a month before I was daring enough to wear it in front of my parents."

"I don't get it. They saw you wear a *kipa* before, didn't they?"

"Sure. But this one had my Hebrew name on it. And they didn't even know I had a Hebrew name. It took me quite a while to work up the nerve to tell them. And the first *kipa* I ever wore—they had a fit when they saw it."

I thought of my own mother and father. "I can imagine," I said.

"My mother—she was the first to see it, and she said, 'What's that old rag doing on your head?' And my father reminded me that I wasn't in some synagogue and I should get rid of it.

"I knew they'd never go along with the religious significance, so I stressed how it was just a symbol of Jewish identity and it was nothing to get excited about." Shimmy paused for a few moments, and then he let out a little laugh. "I guess they couldn't quite go along with that reasoning either. Their symbols of Jewish identity are more along the line of bagels and lox."

"Was that before or after your secret Bar Mitzvah?" I asked him. And then I wondered if I was even supposed to know about his Bar Mitzvah. Was it really a secret? Or only to his mother and father? Then I wondered if he had a Jewish circumcision—a *bris*—and if his parents knew about that.

"That came before," Shimmy said, and he didn't act at all surprised that I knew. "That was before anything. After that came my Bar Mitzvah, and then, using the identity angle, I asked if I could go to the Hebrew high school."

"And they said no."

"Not at first. After I was bugging them about going, they finally said, 'Look—if you want to go to that school, okay. But you do one more religious thing and out you go.' How could I go under those conditions? And now, forget it. They wouldn't even let me near the place."

"You could have gone. You could have done what you wanted to do, and kept it all a secret. Like your Bar Mitzvah."

"Are you kidding? Did you ever try to keep something like that hidden? Well, I tried all right, and let me tell you it's tough."

"Tough? It's impossible. If you want to keep kosher you have to turn into a vegetarian. You've got to sneak off to *shul* like a common criminal and if you want to keep *Shabbos* you practically have to move out of the house."

"Exactly. You sound as if you've experienced it all."

I merely shrugged an answer. But oh, have I ever experienced it. And I was getting tired of the experience, too. I was tired of living from can to can, the contents of which I've had to eat cold most of the time because I was afraid of smelling up the house. And on Saturdays I was tired of pretending to be carsick, and tired of running away from ringing telephones. But mostly I was tired of the excuses. To my mother and father, to Audrey and Roseann. To Aunt Gloria.

"Come on, Heather, I'm taking you out to this great little vegetarian place I've discovered."

"*I can't, Aunt Gloria. It's Saturday. And I don't ride on Saturday.*"

"I'd love to, Aunt Gloria. But my stomach is doing cartwheels, and the thought of getting into the car . . . maybe we can go tomorrow."

"I've got plans for tomorrow, but next Saturday . . ."

What could I tell her? Next Saturday I'll be busy, I'll have a headache, I'll be burning up with fever. And the Saturday after that . . .

I was sick of being a sneak and a liar. I was sick of being a vegetarian.

"The point is," Shimmy was saying, "there's nothing wrong with what I'm doing. And that's what made me decide to bring everything out in the open. I just asked myself, What am I ashamed of? What am I doing that's so wrong, that I have to be secretive about it? Why do I have to hide?"

"You're right," I said. "This isn't the Spanish Inquisition."

"Or Nazi Germany."

"Or Russia. Shimmy, you're doing the right thing," I told him, and I got up. "I'll see you later."

I found Heshy inserting another cassette into Kevin's tape deck. "What time can you come by?" I asked.

He turned and looked at me, his face full of surprise.

"I've decided that I'd like it very much if you went out of your way," I said.

"Great. I'll see you at five."

How would I survive between now and five o'clock next Sunday? That's what I asked Shani when I called her after Kevin's party.

"Maybe your mother and father won't see him," she said.

"Of course they'll see him. My first date! Well, I guess you could call it a date. They'll inspect him up and down. Mostly up. And anyway, I don't know what I'd be afraid of most. That they'll see him and find out, or that they won't see him and won't find out."

"I can understand that last part," she said. "Now that you've psyched yourself up for a confrontation it would be a shame not to have it happen."

"Oh, it'll happen all right, Shani. You can count on it."

14

Timing is all-important. It can work for you or against you. I would not, for example, ask a favor of my father or show him my lousy grades until after he's eaten. And the time to catch my mother would be after she's spent a productive day at the typewriter. Preferably after she's knocked off the last page of a confession. It's all in the timing. And that's why I consider it unfortunate that my mother had to pick the Saturday before "the happening" to get her rejection of "Stowaway."

I found her in a dark mood when I came home from the synagogue. The mood did not put her in the right frame of mind to help accept what she was about to learn. Who knows? A letter of acceptance or a contract, and she might have converted too.

She was reading "Stowaway" when I walked into the house. "Now, what's wrong with this story?" she asked me, pointing to her manuscript. "I'd like to know. At least if they wrote something personal. But no, all they send is this."

She handed me her form rejection, the preprinted kind they send to hundreds of other writers telling them how their manuscripts don't "suit our editorial needs and thank you for thinking of us as possible publishers of your work and good luck elsewhere."

"Oh, don't pay attention to this," I said, handing the rejection back to her. "What do they know?"

"Probably something I don't. Specifically, that I can't write."

"Sure you can. Send it out again. Maybe the next publisher will have better taste."

"Just a form reject. That's all it was worth."

"All great writers get rejected. You told me so yourself."

"Not even a single comment—good story here but we just can't use it, or let's see what else you've written. Nothing."

"And don't forget. You've still got 'Asparagus.'"

"I think I've just about had it," she said, crumpling the rejection and throwing it in the wastebasket.

That really worried me, because up until then she saved the rejections in her scrapbook so she could someday gloat over them.

"I hate to see her this way," I said to Grandpa when I saw him the next day. "She had such high hopes for that story."

"Your mother will bounce back," Grandpa said. "She always does."

"I hope she'll bounce back by five o'clock tonight," I said, and I told him about Heshy. I had to tell him fast—before my father and Shawn came back from the soda machine. All during the telling I pictured my mother and father's reaction when they caught sight of Heshy's *kipa*. Maybe they'd think he came to the wrong house.

"I don't know if I can handle it," I said. "Maybe I should just call the whole thing off."

"And what would you gain by that?" Grandpa asked.

"Time," I said.

"I think maybe too much time has gone by already. And maybe now it's time to bring everything out in the open."

There was a weakness to his voice, and his face looked pale. But he kidded me about my names and asked me who I was today.

"Tell me," he said. "Are you Batsheva or Shira or D'vorah? Or are you back to being Heather?"

"You know something, Grandpa, I don't even know *who* I am."

"In time you will find that out too," he said.

It was almost four o'clock when we got back from visiting Grandpa. I showered—almost slipped in the tub—shampooed my hair, got soap in my eyes, and discovered two new pimples, which I covered up with Clearasil. I dried my hair, put on a plaid skirt and my blue bulky knit, and ran downstairs. Heshy would be here in a few minutes. I would catch him just as he came into sight and run out to meet him. My mother and father could meet him some other time.

Shawn was on the floor looking through a picture book.

"Why don't you ask Mommy to read you the story," I said.

"I don't think she'll want to today. She's mad about *her* story."

"I know. But maybe you can take her mind off it for a while."

"Okay." He got up from the floor and yelled, "Mommy, can you read me a story?"

"No, don't call her from here. Go into the den and tell her. And hurry up before she gets too busy."

I aimed him in the direction of the den and planned my getaway. First my coat. Then as soon as I'd spot Heshy I would yell out a quick "Good-bye I'll see you in a few hours," and get out of the house. I got as far as the closet when I heard my mother's voice.

"Let me see how you look."

I turned around and forced a smile.

"Very pretty," she said. "Now tell me, exactly what kind of concert are they having at school?"

"Sort of a music festival. You know, singing, dancing—the usual. And it's at Shani's school, not mine." My first giant step toward truth.

"A whole bunch of her friends are going," I continued as I put on my coat. "In fact, one of them is coming by for me in a minute or two, so why don't I just go out and wait . . ."

I never got to finish the sentence. The doorbell rang. Neither my mother nor I made a move to answer it.

"Why don't you get that?" she asked. "Or do you want me to?"

"No, that's okay," I said, and sighed. "I may as well." Supreme bravery in the face of death.

I opened the door and sure enough, it was Heshy standing there, looking very handsome and wearing his new *kipa*.

"Hi, Heather. Are you ready?"

"Sure . . . come on in."

By this time my father and Shawn had come to the door to see who it was. And now I had three people staring at a boy with a pot holder on his head. My pot holder.

"Mom, Dad, Shawn, this is Heshy. Heshy Rabinowitz."

"Pleased to meet you," Heshy said, shaking hands with everyone. My mother and father smiled politely, and I could see their eyes shift from Heshy's head to me. I looked away.

"Hmmm, Heshy," my mother said, apparently mulling the name over in her mind, "that's an interesting name. Is it short for something?"

"It's short for Hershel," he said. "I used to be called Hershy."

"Like in Hershey bar?" Shawn asked, and giggled.

Heshy turned to me and grinned. "See what I mean?"

"What English name do you go by?" she asked.

"None," he said. "My parents didn't believe in naming any of us kids in English. We've all got Jewish or Hebrew names."

Another attempt at eye contact. I ignored it again. "I think we'd better go," I said, "or we'll be late."

"You don't have to wait up," I said as we walked out the door. But by the looks on their faces I knew they would.

15

"I'm sorry if they made you feel uncomfortable," I said to Heshy as we began the walk to school. We could have gotten a ride, but I wanted to walk and be alone with him. "I guess it was the *kipa* that threw them."

"You haven't told them much about me, have you?" he asked.

I shook my head. "I haven't told them much about myself either, these past few months. But I have a feeling they'll find out everything after tonight."

"Shimmy all over again, isn't it?"

"Shimmy? Oh, the situation, you mean. Yes, I guess so."

"I had a feeling it was. Well, I went through it

with him, and now it looks like I'll have to go through it with you too."

"Thanks," I said. "I can use the support."

"What's the first thing I can do to help?"

"You can help me pick out a Hebrew name."

"Sure. I'm good at that. How about Shimon, because it means . . ."

"I know, I know, 'hearing, with acceptance.' Thanks just the same, Heshy, but I don't think that name suits me too well."

When we reached the school I found Shani waiting for me at the entrance to the auditorium. She grabbed my arm and pulled me aside.

"So?"

"So?"

"Heather, come on, tell me. How did it go? Did they see him?"

"They saw him all right. And they turned pale and Shawn called him a Hershey bar and . . ."

The music started up and the lights dimmed. "We'd better go in," I said. "I'll tell you everything later."

We ran down the aisle to the front of the auditorium where Heshy and Donald were saving seats for us. I moved in as close to Heshy as I could without getting the arm of the seat stuck in my ribs. He smelled faintly of Mennen skin bracer.

On the stage five guys with guitars, drums, and an electric piano were singing a snappy Hebrew song. And while the drummer pounded away on his drums, thoughts of my homecoming pounded away at my head. And each time they sang a soft, sweet song, such a wave of self-pity came over me that tears welled up in my eyes.

"Are you okay?" Heshy asked.

"I'm very sentimental," I said, and sniffed.

It was only toward the end of the program, when we got up to dance with all the joy and fervor of an Israeli Independence Day celebration, that I was able to put all thoughts of myself in the back of my mind.

After the music festival we went to an Israeli place for pizza and falafel. While I was waiting for the food I went over to say hello to Sunny Margolis, who was sitting at another table. Somehow I got into this whole elaborate introduction of myself so she'd remember who I was.

"Hi, I'm Heather Hopkowitz, Shani Greenwald's friend. The one who wrote you to thank you for the pattern and instructions for making Heshy's *kipa*, the one he's wearing right now."

"I remember you from the *Shabbaton*," she said, putting back the piece of tomato that fell out of her falafel.

"Oh, I didn't know if you would. Thanks again for your help."

"It was nothing. If you want any more patterns, let me know. I've got some nice ones."

She went back to her falafel, and I went back to Heshy. Heshy treated me to the falafel and I treated him to the pizza. I watched Shoshana Katz hanging on to Shimmy, and then Kevin Cornfield drove us home in his station wagon.

"Aren't you afraid to walk home alone in the dark?" I asked Heshy after Kevin dropped both of us in front of my house.

"I'm very brave."

"I'm not." I looked in the direction of the door.

"I'm really sorry I put you in this predicament," Heshy said. "I wish you would have clued me in. I could have waited outside. Or I'd have put on a hat. Even though I hate hats."

He would do that? Heshy Rabinowitz would wear a hat for me? I was beside myself with joy.

"I'm glad you came by for me," I said. "With the *kipa.*"

He took my hand and squeezed it gently. "Good luck in there," he said.

A more platonic gesture than I had hoped for. But nice, and probably just as well considering the possibility that my mother and father were peeking out through the draperies.

Actually they were in the den, pretending to be watching TV. I say pretending because the show that was on was one they consider to be a piece of garbage, and one they'd never watch in a million years.

"Well, well," my father said when I walked in. "Look who's back. How was the concert?"

"Lots of fun," I said, and sat down in a chair across from him and my mother. "And then some of us went out to eat."

"And who are the some of us?" my mother asked.

"Well, let's see. There was Shani, Shoshana, Shimmy . . ."

"What ever happened to Dick and Jane?" my mother asked. "Oh, I'm sorry. Go on."

"And there was Donald and Kevin . . ."

"That's more like it."

"And of course, Heshy."

"He seems very nice."

"He really is."

"And handsome, too. But tell me, does he always wear that . . . that skullcap wherever he goes?"

"I guess so. I've never seen him without one."

She shook her head. "I have never been able to understand why anybody would wear one of those out of the synagogue."

"Because God is all around us. He's everywhere. Not just in a synagogue."

My mother and father exchanged glances. They were probably thinking of taking my temperature.

My father got up to turn the TV off and then he sat down again. "Where did all these new kids come from?"

"I met them while I was staying with Shani. And I've been seeing them pretty often since then."

"All religious?" my mother asked.

"All."

"Well, there's certainly nothing wrong with that. It's good to get exposed to all kinds of people."

Was this my mother talking? The same mother who refused to allow herself to become too close to the Greenwalds because they weren't her kind?

She shifted uneasily in her seat. "I just hope you don't let any of their oddities rub off on you."

I wanted to run upstairs and continue this discussion another time. Like in ten years. But I knew it was now or never.

"I already have let them. Rub off, that is."

They looked at me with faces as blank as a sheet of my mother's white typing paper.

"What did you say?" my father asked.

"I said I've already let their oddities rub off on me."

"What does that mean?"

"I've decided . . . to become . . . religious."

"You what?" my mother cried as she shot up from the couch. "That's ridiculous. I never heard of such a thing."

"Calm down, Abbey. I'm sure she doesn't really mean that."

"I *do* mean it," I said.

"Now, Heather, this is not something you just decide," my father said. "This is a serious matter and it needs to be considered seriously. You need time to think this whole thing over."

"I've had time," I said. "Three months."

"But you don't even realize what's involved. From the outside, religious observance might seem interesting and unique to you. But you don't have any idea what you'd be getting into. I do. I've been there. It's hard living that way."

"Grandma and Grandpa didn't find it hard. Shani doesn't."

"Believe me, it is."

"Not if you like it. Not if you know how." And not if you don't have to live in secrecy, I might have added.

"And you know how, I suppose?"

"I've had practice," I said. "Three months."

"Oh, my God," my mother said, and sank into the nearest chair. "Heather, what are you talking about?"

"Well, I haven't been eating meat here because I'm eating only kosher now."

"You're not a vegetarian?"

"No."

"Oh, my God."

"And I've been going to *shul* every *Shabbos*. And I've given up my Friday night bowling."

"Oh, my God. I knew we should never have gone on that trip. I felt it in my bones. It was the biggest mistake to leave her at that girl's house."

"Let's not overreact," my father said, and began pacing the floor. If he were the drinking type, this would have been the perfect time to open the liquor cabinet and pour himself a shot of something. "You know how kids are. They're always turning on to new things, trying to find out who they are. In time I'm sure she'll get over it."

He was treating me like I had an advanced case of the flu or the chicken pox. "I'm not sick," I said, and I felt my voice grow louder. "There's nothing to get

163

over. I just want to be Jewish. Really Jewish. Why are you getting so upset? You're acting as if I've converted to a whole new religion."

"As far as I'm concerned," said my mother, "it *is* a whole new religion. You might just as well join one of those crazy religious movements for all the difference it makes."

"I'm going to bed."

"No you're not."

"Enough of this," my father said, and started turning off the lights. "We'll talk again tomorrow when we're all in a better frame of mind."

"You bet we'll talk about it again," my mother said. "This subject is far from being closed."

"I won't change my mind," I told her.

"If you want to keep on living here, you will," she said.

They both went up to bed, and I sat in the den, alone in the darkness. We had had our confrontation and it was over. Finished. At least until tomorrow. Was it better than I had expected? Worse? I couldn't figure it out. My head was pounding. But at the same time I felt an overwhelming sense of relief. From now on there would be no more lies. No more hiding. No more health foods. And with that thought, I started toward the stairs and went up to my room. Tomorrow I would dismantle my kitchen.

16

Once when I was eleven years old, I announced to my mother that I no longer wanted to go to Girl Scout camp. She pouted for three days. She always wanted me to be active in the scout movement, the way she used to be. And I wanted it too. At least I thought I did. It was getting hard now for me to sort out what I did for her and what I did for myself.

Anyway, I was reminded of Girl Scout camp very often during the following week, whenever I saw her. She wore a look that seemed to say, What have I done to deserve this? and Where did I go wrong?

My father didn't seem quite as stricken, but I knew it was just a matter of time before he'd try to reason with me. My mother was beyond reason. Her approach was more direct.

165

"Heather," she said at dinner, "I still don't see why you can't eat a hamburger like the rest of us."

"I've got plenty to eat right here," I said. I had heated up a can of beef stew in my pot and ate it with my mother's salad.

"It isn't poison, you know."

"It isn't kosher either."

Shawn looked up from his plate. "What's kosher?" he asked.

"It's nothing," my mother said.

"And how come she's eating from a different dish?"

"Go on and eat."

"He at least ought to know about kosher," I said.

"No thank you. All I need is another religious person in the house."

My father helped himself to his third hamburger. "Shawn will learn about these matters in due time," he said to me.

"What matters?" Shawn asked.

"And don't try to influence him," my mother warned. "Food is food, meat is meat. And I think it's ridiculous to make such a big thing of it."

If meat is meat, why couldn't the meat be kosher? "Do you think maybe we can start buying kosher, as long as we're buying?" I held my breath.

"Heather," my mother said in her supercool voice, "I'm not about ready to go to the trouble of changing my shopping and cooking habits."

"You went through the trouble when I was a vegetarian."

"That was entirely different."

166

"And I'd help you. I would even do the cooking."

"When you move out of here, into your own place, you can do whatever you want," she said, and got up to clear away the dishes.

By Friday I had decided that truth was in order for Audrey and Roseann too.

"So what's your excuse tonight?" Roseann asked me on the way home from school. "No, let me guess. You've got a hot date with some guy you don't want us to know about."

"You're spending the weekend in Teaneck," Audrey said, and pushed her glasses back up off her nose.

"You're sitting for Shawn?" Roseann said.

"You're both wrong," I told them. "My hot date was last week and I've got nothing special planned for tonight."

Roseann slapped me on the back. She almost knocked the wind out of me. "Hey, wow. That means you can go bowling with us. Finally."

"No I can't."

"But you just said . . ."

"I know. But I can't go bowling."

"Why not?"

"I've decided that there are certain things I don't want to do on Friday nights anymore. And bowling is one of them."

"I still don't get it."

"It's no big thing. I'm just trying to be more Jewish, that's all. More observant."

"You're kidding," Roseann said.

"You mean like Shani?" Audrey asked.

I nodded.

"I can't believe it," Roseann said.

"What's so hard to believe?"

"Why on earth would you want to be religious? I mean, I can understand about Shani. She has to. She was born into it. But you've got a choice."

"Well, I guess I've made it then, haven't I?"

"Shani brainwashed you," Roseann said.

"Your new diet doesn't by chance have anything to do with your new religion, does it?" Audrey asked.

I nodded again.

"Oh, brother," Roseann said, shaking her head in disbelief. And she was still shaking it when she and Audrey turned off down the street.

When I got home I changed from my jeans to a skirt and sweater, brought my candles and candleholders down into the dining room, and set them on the table.

"Who's coming to dinner?" Shawn asked.

"Nobody," I said. "These are *Shabbos* candles. I'm going to light them later on."

"What did I tell you about influencing him?" my mother muttered as she brushed past me with her dustcloth.

"I just told him what I was doing," I said.

Shortly before sundown, I heated up the barbecued chicken breast and canned chicken soup that I bought Thursday with my saved-up lunch money and poured myself a tiny glass of grape juice.

168

"Where did all this come from?" my mother asked as she surveyed the dining room table.

"I bought the food yesterday."

"And the candles and holders?"

"I had them up in my room. With the grape juice."

"You used these things before, I take it?"

"Yes."

Her eyes shifted from the table to me. "Now I can understand your sudden need for skirts and sweaters," she said. "In fact, a few other things are starting to come back to me. For instance, who are Batsheva and Malkah?"

"Me," I said. "At least they *were* me. I've been looking around for a Hebrew name."

She shook her head. "I can't believe this. I must be hearing things. All this going on behind our backs. You must have had some good laugh on us, didn't you?"

"I haven't been laughing," I said. "And I only did these things behind your back because I thought you wouldn't understand. And I was right. Because you don't."

"How do you expect me to understand all this nonsense?"

"It's not nonsense," I said.

When my father came home, my mother shot him an expression that said, Just take a look at what's going on here. My father eased her out of the room. I was glad they left so they wouldn't have to go through the pain of watching me light the candles.

I lit the candles, waved my hands over the flames,

and covered my eyes. I silently said the blessing, and barely finished it when I heard, "What's she doing?"

I opened my eyes in time to see my mother pulling Shawn by the arm into the den. "Come and watch TV," she said.

My father poked his head into the dining room and invited me to sit down on the couch with him.

"Heather, I think it's commendable that you want to do this."

I looked at him suspiciously. My father should have been a psychiatrist instead of an oral surgeon.

"Just because I never cared to keep up with any observance doesn't mean you can't."

I heard it but I couldn't believe it. Could it be that he really understood? That his traditional background was catching up with him?

"And if you want to become more involved in religion in the future, fine. I can understand that. But I'm asking you to put off your observance for a while."

"Put it off?"

"That's right. Until you're grown and out on your own."

"But that's not fair," I said. I remembered what Shani said about observance being a way of life. How could I put off a way of life?

"I can't put it off," I told him. "It's a way of life."

"You could do it for us if you really wanted to."

"Do it for you? What about me? Don't I have anything to say about how I want to live my life? And what am I doing that's so wrong? You're acting like I'm into drugs or I've joined a crazy religious cult or something."

"I'm not saying that what you're doing is wrong. It just creates a conflict right now. You know how your mother feels."

"Yeah. She has a religious hang-up."

"Heather, I don't want you talking that way about your mother."

"Well, it's true, you know. She's ashamed of anything—or anyone—that's too Jewish. It rubs her the wrong way."

"Your mother has never had any kind of Jewish upbringing, and then you throw something like this at her. What do you expect?"

"She can still try to understand me. Mom likes to think of herself as an open-minded and liberal person. Why can't she open her mind to me and what I'm doing?"

My father put his arm around me. "You've always been her girl, you know."

"I still am."

"Not in the same way. This changes things for her. You've adopted a whole new way of living and thinking that she can't go along with."

"I don't know what I can do about that," I said.

My father heaved a sigh and stood up. "Well, I can see that we're not going to get anywhere right now. I just hope you'll think about what I've said."

I did think about it. I thought about it long enough

171

to know he was trying to make me feel guilty. It wasn't going to work. I felt lousy, maybe. But not guilty.

After lunch on Saturday, I was sitting on the floor playing a game of checkers with Shawn. The phone rang. I ignored it.

"Will someone get that?" my mother called from the bathroom.

Shawn ran into the kitchen, pulled up a chair, climbed onto the table, and reached for the phone.

"Hello?" he said.

My mother walked into the kitchen. "Who is it?"

"I don't know. They hung up."

"Oh, Heather," my mother said. "You know how long it takes for him to answer the phone. Why couldn't you have gotten it?"

"I don't answer the phone on Saturday."

"I've just about had it with you," she said, throwing her hands up in the air. "Why you choose to live this way is beyond me. I don't even know you anymore. You're turning into a religious fanatic."

So what? I thought. There are all kinds of fanatics in this world. Roseann is a bowling fanatic, Aunt Gloria is a health food fanatic, and my mother is a writing fanatic. So what's wrong with a religious fanatic?

"You should be grateful to me," I said. "Now you can have something really good to write about. You can write about something you know. None of this 'Stowaway' and 'Asparagus' stuff. You can write about your daughter, the religious fanatic. I even have a title for you. 'How My Daughter Left Me for God.'"

I put on my coat and went to seek refuge at Shani's house.

"I'm sorry it's working out this way," she said when I related the events of the week to her.

"I think my mother's about ready to disown me."

Shani smiled. "The next thing you know she'll say *kaddish* over you."

Kaddish—the mourner's prayer. "Yes, she probably would—if it wasn't such a Jewish thing to do."

On Tuesday I walked home from school with Audrey and Roseann, who were singing the new senior class song. The music and lyrics were original—they were even more original when sung by Audrey and Roseann. Roseann kept singing off-key, and Audrey forgot most of the words.

"Hey, you're not singing," Roseann said to me just after *Now the world outside is calling*. "Where's your school spirit?"

"I don't know. I guess I don't have any today." Something was bothering me. It wasn't the religious problem. It was something inside of me that was making me feel uneasy, and I didn't know what it was. All I knew was that I felt this need, this urgency to get home. For some reason, I knew I had to be there.

From the corner I could see my father's car in the driveway. Something was definitely wrong. He never comes home so early in the day. Maybe something happened to him. Or to my mother—or to Shawn. I ran all the way to the house. My hands wouldn't

173

work and I couldn't find the key, so I rang the bell.

My father opened the door. His face was gray, almost the color of the coat he was wearing. My mother was putting on her own coat and Shawn was standing next to her.

"What's wrong?" I asked, trying to catch my breath. "Where's everybody going?"

"It's Grandpa," my father said. "He's had another stroke. They've taken him to the hospital."

"I'm going with you," I said, and dropped my books on the table.

"You'd better stay here and watch Shawn," my mother said. "We'll call you if anything . . ."

"I'm going with you," I insisted.

We dropped Shawn off at a neighbor's and got in the car. We drove to the hospital in silence, my mother and father in front, and me in the back hoping and praying, Dear God, please let him get out of it. Don't let him die. Please, dear God, don't let him die.

These words were with me all the way to the hospital and all the way up in the elevator to the fourth floor. A nurse accompanied my mother and father to Grandpa's room, and I was asked to remain in the waiting room.

I walked over to the window and looked out across the park. The days were longer now. Spring was officially here. Passover—*Pesach*—would be here in just three weeks. Three weeks. Maybe with a miracle Grandpa would be better by then. I could come visit him and we could have a seder. Just the two of us. A real seder with matzo and wine. And the Cup of Elijah. . . .

"*Whose glass is that big one, Grandpa?*"

"*Why, that's Elijah's cup. Every* Pesach, *Elijah the prophet comes into every Jewish home that has a seder, and drinks from the cup that's put out especially for him. So go on, Heather, open the door and let Elijah in.*"

"*I can't see him.*"

"*He's invisible. But he's there.*"

"*Look, Grandpa, the wine's moving. He's drinking from his cup.*"

"*I think you're right, Heather. There's not as much as before.*"

"*Why doesn't he drink it all, Grandpa?*"

"*If he drank all the wine people left for him, imagine how drunk he would get. So it's just a sip before he goes on to the next house.*"

"*Is he finished?*"

"*Yes, he's finished. I think he's gone now. You can close the door.*"

"*I don't want him to be gone, Grandpa. I want him to come back.*"

"*He will . . . next year. But now he's gone. . . .*"

"He's gone, Heather." I felt a hand on my shoulder and turned around to see my father. "Your grandpa is gone."

17

The funeral took place on Wednesday. I'm not sure how much of it I remember. Mostly I remember feelings—a terrible sadness, a numbness, a certain amount of fear for Grandpa, a desperate attempt to gain comfort from the words "He lived a long life, a good life."

Right after the funeral, we picked up Shawn from his friend's house and went home to get ready for my father's period of *shiva*. That seven-day period when friends and relatives come to offer comfort and support to the bereaved. The way it was when Mr. Teitlebaum died. But it was not that way at all.

"You're supposed to drape the mirrors," I told my mother.

"Superstitious nonsense," she said, and lost no time in putting out the liquor and otherwise preparing for the guests. She ordered Chinese food for dinner—extra in case some of the guests would want some. And of course there was coffee, cake and fruit, and candy dishes filled with M&M's.

As the guests began to arrive, she went flitting around the house, answering the door, hanging up coats, and encouraging everyone to help themselves to food and drink—which they did almost as soon as the words "I'm sorry" were offered to my father, who alternated between sitting and walking around the room. Shawn seemed to be having more fun that night than he had at his own birthday party.

All evening long they came, and the talking grew louder and louder, and there was laughing and joke-telling. My grandfather was dead, and they were having a party and eating egg foo yung. I took as much of it as I could, and then I went upstairs to my room.

I spent the next half hour or so lying on my bed, fingering the paperweight that Shani had given me when she heard about Grandpa. Inside the glass were several blades of grass, along with a saying from the Psalms.

> Man's days are like grass;
>   he blooms like the flower of the field.
> A wind passes by and it is no more,
>   its own no longer knows it.

There was a knock on the door, and my father walked into the room.

"Hi. Are you all right?"

"I'm okay."

"Why don't you come down and join us?"

"I don't think so."

"It might be better than being alone."

I shook my head. "I'm not in the mood for a party."

My father got red in the face and his nostrils flared. I had never seen him like that before.

"A party? Heather, don't you realize what's happened? We just buried your grandfather, and you're talking about a party?"

"Don't *I* realize? Dad, close your eyes for a moment. Close your eyes and listen."

"Heather . . ."

"I mean it. Close your eyes and listen to what's going on down there."

For a moment he stood there, listening. He didn't even have to close his eyes.

"Do you hear it?"

Without answering, he rushed out of the room. I followed him downstairs where he gathered up the bottles of liquor and put them back in the liquor cabinet. Then he put away all the bottles of soda and the M&M's.

My mother hurried over to him and tried to stop him. "Harvey, what are you doing?"

"What does it look like I'm doing?"

"But most of the people are still here."

"Yes they are. But it seems they've forgotten what they're here for." He stopped what he was doing and looked straight at her. "And apparently so have we, Abbey. Now I'd like you to tell those loud-mouthed friends of yours to shut up."

"Harvey . . ."

"And I want you to sit down. No more running around the house. And no more catered affairs. Nothing. Not even a pot of coffee."

For the next six days, my mother didn't cater any more affairs. But she kept the coffee urn on the table.

When the week was up, my father and I went to the convalescent home to pick up Grandpa's things.

"I'm coming with you to see Grandpa," Shawn said to me.

"He won't be there, Shawn. Remember, we told you that Grandpa died? And last week was the funeral?"

"Like we had when my hamster died?"

"Yes, sort of."

"That means we won't ever see Grandpa again."

"That's right, Shawn. But we'll always remember him."

Grandpa had his own remembrances tucked away in his room. Photographs, papers, books. And among his books there was a small, white, satin-covered Bible. I opened it up, and on the inside of the front cover I saw something written in Hebrew.

"What does this say?" I asked my father.

"Let me see," he said, and looked over my shoulder. "It's your grandmother's name. Chana Hopkowitz."

"Her name was Chana?"

"It was her Hebrew name. But Grandpa was the only one who called her that. To everyone else she was Hannah."

"I wish he'd told me," I said. "I wish I'd known." All those wasted weeks of searching for a name, and it was right here all the time.

I held the Bible close to me. And then I looked at the name again. My name. Me. Chana Hopkowitz.

18

When I told Shani how I came to call myself Chana (like *Chanukah* and *l'chayim*, the *ch* is pronounced like you're clearing your throat), she didn't question the name at all.

"It's a pretty name," she said. "A meaningful name. I like it."

She introduced me as Chana to all the kids at the synagogue on Saturday, and Heshy said, "You know something, Chana? You look like a Chana."

"Chana means 'grace,' " I said, "so I'll take that as a compliment."

To Audrey, who still couldn't decide about her hair or her contacts, and to Roseann, and of course to my mother and father, I was still Heather. But it was

Chana who had the courage to ask my mother a question that Heather might not have dared to ask.

"Can we have a seder this year?" I asked it just after she stuffed her "Asparagus" into a manila envelope. I thought the timing was right.

"We always have one," she said.

"We never have a seder," I said. "We have a Passover dinner."

Passover dinner. With your choice of bread or matzo, wine that isn't even kosher, no reading of the *Haggadah*, which tells the story of Passover, and a table full of strangers who couldn't care less about the holiday.

"I thought we might have an authentic seder—like Grandma and Grandpa used to have. And just with the family. Us and Aunt Gloria, if she wants to come."

"Heather, if you want an authentic seder, why don't you just invite yourself to Shani's house?"

For the first time since the conversation began, my father looked up from his paper and interrupted us.

"If she wants a seder that much, she should be able to have one in her own home."

"I wouldn't even know where to begin."

"And it's not a bad idea, either. They were always a lot of fun for me as a kid. I remember how much I looked forward to them every year."

"All that ceremony. I can't see any point to it."

"And Shawn has never been to a real seder. I'd like him to experience one."

"It just seems so complicated."

182

"Heather and I will take care of everything. Won't we, Heather?"

During the week, my father and I went to the supermarket and bought Passover food in the section that was set up especially for the holiday. We bought a few pots and pans and plastic-coated paper plates so we wouldn't have to bother with new dishes. "Maybe next year," my father said. Then we went to the liquor store for some Carmel wine.

"How about Shawn?" I asked. "Should we get some grape juice for him?"

"Let him live a little," my father said. "We'll give him the real thing. But just a tiny glass."

When we got home, my father checked the Yellow Pages for a nearby kosher meat market, and picked up the telephone.

"Just tell me what you want, and I'll have them deliver," he said to my mother.

"Harvey . . ."

"It's just as easy to throw a kosher chicken in the pot as a non-kosher one."

"Oh, for heaven's sake," she said, and took the phone away from him so she could place the order herself.

I spent the next few days getting the kitchen ready for Passover. I cleaned out all the cabinets, getting rid of any bread and cookie crumbs that were around, and set aside one cabinet for the Passover food. I washed out the refrigerator, and my mother agreed to let me have a few shelves that I could use in there too. And while I was cleaning, I taught Shawn the

Four Questions that the youngest family member is supposed to ask at the seder.

"Okay, Shawn," I said, just after I sprayed out the oven, "let me hear what you know so far."

He got down from the sink, where he had been splashing around in some soapsuds, and came over to me.

"Why is this night different from all other nights?" he began. "On all other nights we eat leavened bread. . . . What's leavened bread, Heather?"

"That's regular bread. I told you. Remember?"

"Oh, yeah. On all other nights we eat leavened bread or matzo. What's matzo?"

"That's what's in that box I showed you. It's sort of a cracker."

"Oh, yeah. On all other nights we eat leavened bread or matzo. On this night we only eat matzo. That's all I know."

"That's perfect. Only three more questions to go. Oh, Shawn," I said, and stooped down to hold his wet little body close to me, "just wait until the seder. It'll be so much fun. We'll read a story from the *Haggadah* and we'll sing songs, and best of all, we'll open the door for Elijah."

"Who's Elijah?"

"He's the prophet who comes to everyone's seder. We'll pour wine in his own special cup and then we'll open the door for him and he'll come in and drink the wine and we won't be able to see him because he's invisible."

"If he's invisible, how do we know he's there?"

"We'll know, all right. He's always there."

One of the last things I had to do in the kitchen, and the hardest, was to scour the burners on top of the stove. I took some steel wool and scrubbed until my fingers were scratched and red. The next thing I knew, my mother was standing next to me. Without saying anything, she picked up a piece of steel wool and started on another burner.

"Next year we'll call an oven-cleaning service," she said.

I smiled at her.

"Don't expect me to change with you."

"I don't."

"I suppose we can set aside one of the cabinets for your things . . . and buy kosher meat once in a while."

"Thanks, Mom," I said, and gave her a hug.

I soaked and polished our everyday silverware, and then on the day of the seder, I helped my mother with the cooking and set the table.

My father was practicing his singing while he arranged the Passover plate with all the symbols of the holiday on it. Symbols that included the bitter herbs, the salt water, and my favorite, the green vegetable. A sign of spring; a sign of hope. A wineglass was set at each plate, a *Haggadah*, and in the center of the table, the cup of Elijah. A silver cup that had been my grandfather and grandmother's.

Aunt Gloria arrived, bearing a basket of fruit, and when evening came, we gathered around the table and my father started the seder.

185

Shawn stood up, holding his *Haggadah*, his sweet face catching the glow of the candlelight, and began, "Why is this night different from all other nights?"

Oh, Shawn, I thought. How can I ever begin to tell you?

Temple Israel

Minneapolis, Minnesota

In Honor of the Bat Mitzvah of
DEBRA GENE BLUMENTHAL
by
Her Parents

March 27, 1982